BODY IN SPACE

A RITA PATEL MYSTERY

By Catherine Cooper

Typeset and published by
Oxford eBooks Ltd.
www.oxford-ebooks.com

Oxford eBooks

Introduction

*"Space isn't remote at all. It's only an hour's drive away
if your car could go straight upwards."*

Fred Hoyle, 1979

Sunday, 20th July 2014 4pm

"He could be going anywhere!" Rita Patel exclaims to her brother, putting her foot down on the accelerator of the Peugeot as the motorbike they are following gathers speed.

"What if he's going to the motorway?" she asks anxiously, thinking out loud.

"At least we'll know." Nayan, aged 16, two years younger than his sister and eager to be old enough to learn to drive himself, retorts from the passenger seat.

"There! Take that turning!" Nayan points urgently to the side road taken by the biker.

They find themselves in the winding lanes at the back of the village of Blaby in Leicestershire, having left the busy Narborough Road and the centre of Leicester behind them. The bike rider seems to know where he's going and to be oblivious of the red car pursuing him.

Rita had collected Nayan from the National Space Centre as directed by her parents ("If we are going to insure you, you have to do your fair share of ferrying your brother about."). Their parents were especially anxious since Nayan and his friend had been attacked recently in the city centre.

Just as they had pulled away from the car park, Nayan had shouted.

"There! Look! There's one of the gang that beat me up! Quick, follow him!"

Rita had not had time to argue but has been trying to raise an objection ever since, when she can find the brain space in between looking out for other vehicles and keeping an eye on the direction the bike is taking. Rita passed her driving test only a few months ago and racing through busy streets chasing a motor bike had not been one of the skills tested.

The radio is on in the Peugeot, the strong beat of Beyonce's performance being replaced by local news; but neither occupant pays any attention. Had they done so they would have heard among the items "A body has been found in the River Soar. It is believed to be that of a woman. The police are not releasing any further details at present."

"How can you be sure it's the one who attacked you?" she asks her brother as she changes up the gears. "They all look the same don't they? Long hair and tattoos?"

"He has a skull and cross bones on his helmet, he dropped it on the ground when he came over to speak to us, and before he attacked me, and his bike has an England flag."

"Is that all?" Rita is not sure if the possibility that they are following the wrong man makes her more or less worried.

"I know it's him, all right?" Nayan is insistent.

"What do we do if we catch up with him? What if he's with his gang and they get nasty?" Rita says. She was told to bring Nayan home, not to chase around the county with him, she thinks.

"We won't confront them, silly!" Nayan is dismissive. "If we can just get close enough we'll take some pictures, maybe film him, then we can show the police!"

"There!" Nayan points as the bike takes the left fork at a T-Junction. "He's heading towards Broughton Astley."

"What's there?" Rita shouts above the Peugeot engine as she negotiates the junction.

"We'll find out." says her younger sibling confidently.

The hedged fields go by in a flash of green, interspersed with farm gates and trees. The sun is still high in the sky and flashes between the foliage like a strobe light making it hard for Rita to focus on the road never mind the bike. Fortunately the engine of their quarry is very distinctive so she can hear it ahead and Rita allows a bit of a gap to develop between them in case he notices that the same car has taken his route ever since he left Leicester. The road widens and they emerge in the village of Broughton Astley. It had once been a small backwater, with a single shop, church and village hall but with all the development that has taken place in the last 30 years the place has expanded and now has a series of housing estates and a population in excess of 6,000.

St Mary's church sits back from the road, serenely separate from the traffic and the spreading housing. A few farmer's cottages give way to 1970s box-style homes, 1980s houses in a neo-Georgian style and more contemporary constructions in red brick with sloping roofs and velux windows to maximise the use of the space. The ratio of house size to garden area varies. Front gardens are well-tended, back gardens are peopled with squealing children, many bouncing on garden trampolines while contented looking householders stride up and down with lawnmowers.

This scenery is lost on Rita and Nayan, their focus fixed on the fate of the phantom biker who seems to have disappeared.

"Try there" Nayan suggests indicating a side turning to an industrial estate. Rita signals left and soon finds herself at a derelict landscape of empty buildings with a large 'To Let' sign in one corner; caravans can be seen backing on to the site. Both sign and buildings have seen better days.

The good news is that the sister and brother know they have made the right decision as they can see the motorbike leaning on its stand not far from the 'To Let' sign. The bad news is that the bike is not alone, and therefore neither is its owner. There are two more bikes, and all the riders are huddled in a tense circle, like footballers discussing how to take a penalty kick.

"I'll get my phone from my bag." says Rita and before Nayan can speak she pulls up and leaps out of the driver's seat to go to the back of the car to lift the hatch and take out her red Cath Kidston bag. What Rita does not see is one of the bikers bearing down on the car, intent on breaking the car's window with a baseball bat. As Rita appears from her side of the car to open the hatch he brings down the baseball bat with full force but instead of the glass of the window it is Rita's head that it strikes.

Sunday, 20th July 2014 5.30pm

Rita is drifting in space, floating in a dark expanse. She does not have a space suit, she does not seem to need one. Those suits she and her friend Priya had seen on their visit to the Space Centre, with their intricate engineering for bodily functions, were unnecessary after all! You could just glide above the earth; it was as easy as swimming, easier really because there was no resistance! Rita thinks. Her body feels light, the equipment around her is spinning. Looking down, Rita is amazed to see she is leaving large white footprints, just like the ones painted on the path to the National Space Centre! This must be what happens when you go space walking! What was that female astronaut called? Rita tries to get her brain back to earth. Maureen Cummings? (No, that wasn't right, that was someone else; she hadn't gone into space had she?) Helen Sharman, that was the one; the first and only British woman to go into space. Her suit and some of her equipment were at the Space Centre.

Rita, gaining consciousness, hears the roaring engine of the ambulance she is travelling in as it races through the streets of Leicester, then the sound of someone sobbing, which, as she concentrates, turns out to be herself. Opening her eyes she is assailed by a bright light which someone is shining at her pupils, carefully watching how they react.

"Good to have you back with us." the tall paramedic, a man of about 40 with receding fair hair and wearing a green jumpsuit, utters these words in what Rita thinks may be an

Australian accent, but she cannot be sure. Rita, disappointed not to be in orbit, she was quite enjoying the feeling, thinks about raising her head but realises the effort would be too much. Across from her, on the other side of the ambulance, she is aware of a crouching figure whom she recognises but whose name eludes her. Is it a friend from sixth form? Is it a relative? How has this happened anyway? In contrast to the fast speed at which the vehicle is travelling, Rita's brain reaches slowly to make any sense of her circumstances, to provide a narrative for her present predicament, but only snapshots of events appear, like the 'previously on' segments which precede the next episode of a long running television series. And then the screen goes blank again.

Arriving at the Royal Infirmary, Rita comes round enough to hear the ambulance doors open and feels the air from the outside world come rushing in. The trolley moves, she is flying along but this time she knows she is being propelled by wheels and willing hands. She hears her name just as, embarrassingly, an overwhelming urge to vomit overtakes her and nature takes its course. There are times when gravity comes in useful, she thinks ruefully, as most of the material is skilfully caught by a nurse bearing a grey cardboard bowl.

"Sorry." she manages to mutter.

"Not to worry, it's what we're here for." says the doctor who orders a CT scan.

Monday, 21ˢᵗ July 2014 10am

Rita has had the CT scan. The process resembled nothing so much as being asked to put your head in the door of a large washing machine, or so it seemed to Rita. Not that she had ever laid her head in the door of a washer of course. But the machine was a large white circle with lights and Rita imagined she could almost smell Persil so powerful was the similarity; it was like being asked to lie on the floor of a launderette.

Now Rita's whole body is approaching the inside of another machine and she feels like she is floating again, weightless, gliding on her back towards a white capsule. Soon she is enclosed in the machine, where the darkness and the silence are absolute. Lying on her back in a hospital gown, clutching the emergency alarm in case she has an emergency ("But try not have one," the radiographer had said as she settled her on the sliding mechanism). Then a disembodied voice from nowhere is talking into her earphones - "Okay, Rita ready to start, this one is 4 minutes" - and a noise begins, a clattering, jarring noise, like a pneumatic drill.

Rita shuts her eyes and lets the hammering carry on as if it does not affect her. Except she finds she picks up the rhythm and music to that beat filters into her mind. The song 'Titanium' echoes around in her head, which she tries to expel ("No metal allowed in the MRI scanner" she remembers the radiographer said). The hammering stops. The voice returns "Okay, Rita. Well done. This one is one and a half minutes." Another type of Morse code starts tapping away like a demented wood pecker. Morse code? Rita recalls there is a puzzle she is supposed to solve. Why is she trying to solve it? Is it a school project? Surely not; hasn't she left school now her A-levels are done? Letters and numbers dance around in her mind as the banging noise continues, each figure is trying to find its place in the dance, the letters and numbers are swimming together and splitting apart until…

"The next one's five minutes." the voice intones, but Rita hardly notices what the voice says or registers the next version of tap dancing in her ears. The moving figures have settled into a pattern and Rita has solved the puzzle. Now she knows the answer, all she has to do is to remember what the question is, and why it is important, and tell someone.

Around Rita's bed at the Leicester Royal Infirmary, wearing concerned expressions, are her mother, Padma, and father, Jahi. They have placed their chairs together and are holding hands to comfort each other. Opposite them, on the other side of the bed, sitting by a stack of monitors which are displaying various numbers and patterns, is their youngest child, Nayan, his face twisted in anguish.

"Wake up Rita." Nayan whispers to her. "This is all my fault, wake up!"

"You know she won't." Jahi says sharply, "Not for quite a while. They have put her in a coma so her brain can have a rest and hopefully the swelling will go down. She took quite a crack on the head."

"I know." says Nayan close to tears.

"But you were very brave to rescue her." his mother's tone is soft as she comes over to Nayan's side of the bed to put her arm round him, "Even if you did take quite a risk." she adds.

"I don't know what you were both thinking." says Jahi sharply, frowning again as he recalls Nayan's description of events; how, when his sister had been struck, he, Nayan had pushed Rita's crumpled body into the back of the car, had lept into the driver's seat and put the Peugeot into gear before screeching away from the site, dreading that the motorbikes would appear in the rear-view mirror. ("I didn't know you knew how to drive." Padma had said to her son, too shocked to take it all in.) As soon as it seemed safe, Nayan had pulled in near a row of houses and called 999, breathing for the first time in at least five minutes, or so it had seemed.

***

There are other visitors to Rita's bedside in the next days, visitors of whom she is unaware as she sleeps on, like a

Disney princess, subdued by the effects of morphine.

"Oh Rita." says her best friend from sixth form, Priya Shah, "I am so sorry. I feel that this is all my fault." and the boy sitting next to her squeezes Priya's hand for comfort.

"Can't wait for you to come round, I miss you, but I wouldn't say so if you could hear me." This is Mohal, her older brother, who stands at the foot of her bed, his tall figure casting a long shadow over it.

"Rita." says her friend and former employer Athena Maitland, tossing back her auburn hair in agitation as she rests her clasped hands on the bed "Please wake up. I should never have asked you to help."

"Oh Rita." says her friend Richard Gregson who has been taken to the Infirmary by a careworker from his residential home "I am sorry to see you in this state. I do hope I am not responsible." he says as he sits by her side in his wheel chair.

"Well, Rita," says a rotund middle-aged policeman in uniform, taking off his hat and sitting down beside her on a blue hospital chair. "The sooner you get better the sooner you can tell me what's been going on and I promise to listen this time."

Chapter

1

"We choose to go to the moon in this decade and do the other things, not because they are easy, but because they are hard, because that goal will serve to organize and measure the best of our energies and skills, because that challenge is one that we are willing to accept, one we are unwilling to postpone, and one which we intend to win, and the others, too."

John F Kennedy, 1962

Tuesday, 1st July 2014 3.30pm

Nineteen days before a baseball bat collides with Rita Patel's head, a man walks determinedly across the white boot prints which represent the steps of an astronaut and are painted on the tarmac path leading to the National Space Centre. In his anxiety he is oblivious to the footprints and makes one small step through the entrance as the sliding doors give a satisfying 'swish' like the sound of the doors on the Starship Enterprise.

The man, who is black, with short hair and a square shaped earring in his right ear lobe, wears a dark jacket over jeans and a green sweatshirt. He has a blue cap pulled down low on his head which he hopes will guard his face from any CCTV. The man produces his annual pass from his backpack. He uses this to enter the exhibition area, placing the barcode on the silver turnstile gate. The man looks at his watch, he is early. He walks confidently to the Sir Patrick Moore Planetarium, the largest planetarium in Europe it says on the leaflet he collected at the entrance. At weekends the tickets are checked to see if the entrant has a booking for the specific performance of the show, but today is quieter and the assistants are talking together, so he strolls in unchallenged, the back pack slung over his right shoulder. The man's eyes have just adjusted to the lighting when it dims, like the lights going down on the TV show *Who Wants to be a Millionaire?* He puts the backpack down on the seat next to him. Along the row he notices a party of older people, chattering together like excited children.

The visual effects are spellbinding as the audience bend their necks to gaze upward. The whole of the area above their heads is filled with images and colours, like a brilliant firework display; there are stars, planets, and ideas of what aliens might look like. The voiceover states how, although it is possible there is other life in space, many (including Professor Brian Cox who is reported to have said that alien life is all but impossible) are sceptical that life could exist elsewhere in our galaxy. What the scientists are looking for are planets where the conditions for life could exist, of which water and temperature (the Goldilocks effect) are deemed important. The man gazes mesmerised at the presentation, his eyes and ears fully engaged. No such planets have been detected but space travel takes many years so it is a long time before data can be obtained. A spacecraft is on its way now to a comet, the presentation tells them, to examine what material is spinning around in space and whether it could sustain life. The Rosetta mission, run by the European Space Agency, launched their craft 10 years ago and it is due to land on a comet (if the team can achieve this) later on in the year.

Eventually, to the man's disappointment, the show draws to a close. The man rises from his seat and reaches across for the bag he left next to him. It is not there. Panic seizes the man, starting in his stomach and spreading through arms and legs to hands and feet, which begin the tremble. He tries to push down the feeling, to tell himself he must be mistaken Maybe he put the bag down somewhere else? He gets on his knees to search under and around the chairs as the rest of the Planetarium audience exits. The more he looks, the greater the level of anxiety he feels.

Tuesday, 1*st* July 2014 8.30pm

Later, the man wonders why, when people bang their heads in animated films, they are shown seeing stars. Being propelled by fists around the confines of the disabled toilet at the Space Centre, all he can see is his own pained image reflected in the glass of the mirrors against which his face and body are being pressed. The sensations he feels are an empty, painful, ache in his chest, where a blow has knocked the air out of his lungs, a numbness in his face, where a fist has connected with a cheek bone, and an agonising feeling in his shoulder, where his arm is being pinned back, his face squashed against the wavy edges of the mirrors.

Threats are issued in agitated voices; the general atmosphere is one of panic and the air of unpredictability makes the situation all the more frightening. The man is unable to call out for help, even if aid were at hand, as tape has been applied to his mouth. The inability to take in gulps of air is adding to the discomfort in his chest. Another blow lands and still he does not see stars, only darkness.

Thursday, 3*rd* July 2014 9am

Rita's school friend, Priya, smiles up at Ben Cohen, a friend from Year 13, as they meet at the entrance to Leicester Royal Infirmary in accordance with their Facebook messaging the previous day. Priya has her straight brown black hair tied with a white ribbon into a pony tail which sits elegantly down the back of the white shirt she wears with black trousers, aiming for a look which is smart but not too formal. Ben is over six feet tall,has collar length brown hair with a long fringe which he flicks when he is thinking; today he is clad in tight light brown cords, which hug his legs, and a blue short sleeve shirt. Ben's father, a Home Office pathologist, has agreed they can witness a post-mortem.

Priya (who needs 120 points from her A-levels to take up her offer go to Merton College, Oxford, to study the preclinical part of the 6 year medicine course) was thrilled to be asked. Ben, who has been studying the same subjects as Priya and is also set on having a medical career, has an offer from St John's College, Cambridge. In Ben's case this career choice is not a surprise as, not only is his father a pathologist, his grandfather was a surgeon. For Priya's family her intentions are a new departure. Her parents are in sales (her mother runs an internet clothing business and her father sells computers); neither went to university and nor did her older sister, Meera, who left school after her GCSEs and is now working as a PA. Meera is intimidated by her sibling's cleverness ("I don't know where Priya gets her brains from," she says).

The aspiring medical students descend in a lift to the pathology lab and mortuary where the corridors are quiet and business-like compared to the hubbub of the main hospital above them, and people go about their work without rushing or the sense of urgency which seems to punch through the air of the main hospital corridors. Here the subjects of inquiry are not whole people but tissue and cells. Several figures in the laboratories they pass can be seen carrying out tests, dispensing liquids with syringes and noting down results. The atmosphere is calm and most people are dressed like workers in a food factory, in white overalls, some, but not all, also wear hats to cover their hair. Priya assumes this is to prevent contamination of samples or evidence.

Ben seems to know his way around ("Dad lets me come in at weekends sometimes") and leads the way through swing doors, then turns left and opens another door, waiting for Priya to go through first. They are in a sort of enclosed viewing platform, the nearest analogy Priya can think of is with a box at the theatre. Appropriate, she thinks, since they are to witness events in an operating theatre environment. A shape lies on a trolley, covered by a sheet. It is clear to Priya that this is the body to be examined. She experiences a shiver of excitement, thinking through in her head the various steps taken in a post-mortem. An assistant is preparing the room for Professor Cohen, a tall man who enters wearing green scrubs, gloves and boots. He nods upwards to them and says through the microphone link to the box, "Hi Ben, hi Priya. Glad you could make it!"

The white male assistant uncovers the body and Ben's father begins a commentary which Priya knows will be recorded and transcribed. The body is a black male, IC3 in the police code, which Professor Cohen uses, meaning African or Afro Carribean. He appears to Priya to be about 30 and Professor Cohen cautiously intones that he appears to be somewhere between 25 and 35 years old. "Identity unknown." he adds ('That's interesting' Priya thinks and files away the information to tell Rita, who likes mysteries). "Body found yesterday," the Professor hesitates while he checks his notes, "that's Wednesday second July, in the Mercury Capsule in the National Space Centre." he speaks with a puzzled expression which Priya thinks justified (Rita will be fascinated when she tells her!) "the toxicology will be the key" the pathologist adds. "Apparent suicide. Heroin overdose….So let's see."

Priya watches with fascination as Professor Cohen methodically examines the body with his eyes, looking carefully and noting anything unusual. The man's height and weight are recorded (the assistant has this information ready for the Professor) and he is pronounced to have no distinguishing marks, scars or tattoos on the front of his body. But there are external features which draw the attention of the Professor. He speaks of bruising around the ribs and on the face and he looks carefully for any injection sites, not finding any on the arms or the feet as he seems to have been expecting. Ben's father summarises the overall condition of the corpse; "Well, the body looks to be in good condition, if rather under - nourished, so far as I can tell from an external examination. No obvious track marks or signs of frequent injecting which you would expect if he was an addict. Obviously the toxicology will tell us more. We've taken hair samples?" the assistant nods "I've sent them off" he says.

"Okay." says Professor Cohen, "We'll do blood next, but before we do I would say that there are some disturbing marks on the body. Can you take a close-up please?" – the assistant leans over the supine body to oblige as Ben's father points to certain places and intones "Some bruising to the torso. This suggests ante-mortem collision with an object most likely a fist." he says ('So he was in a fight' thinks Priya). "Let's turn him over before we do anything else." the pathologist says and he and the assistant turn the body onto his stomach, exposing the back, buttocks and the back of his legs and head. Somehow to Priya this makes the scene more shocking and upsetting; the man has lost whatever dignity he seemed to have while he lay on his back just looking like he was asleep. But she can see the usefulness of what the Professor has done.

"Hmmn." Professor Cohen crowds closely over the body as does the assistant. "You see that?" the Professor asks, and the assistant nods and takes more pictures. Priya is curious to know what they can see. Finally Professor Cohen satisfies her curiosity.

"Some burn marks. Cigarette burns I would say. Ante-mortem. Looks like our friend was in some sort of trouble before he went to meet his maker." he says.

The two men turn the body onto its back again. "You combed the hair?" Professor Cohen checks, and nods towards the short hair on the head of the body. "Yes, Professor, nothing untoward in his hair." the assistant, who Priya notes has an Irish accent, confirms. The Professor then draws several blood samples which the assistant labels for the laboratory.

"Now we'll have a look inside." says Professor Cohen, starting up the electric saw.

"Pay special attention Ben and Priya." he tells them "There is always more to learn. No two bodies are put together exactly the same. I've had bodies with their hearts on the wrong side. That scared me until I realised; enlarged livers, multiple nipples, you name it, it's amazing we call anything normal, really."

He begins the Y-shaped incision from the shoulders, joining at the breast bone and extending down to the pubic bone. This enables him to peel back the skin to expose the underlying tissue and organs, the ribcage and the abdominal cavity. Priya is entranced and she can see Ben is fascinated too.

One by one, like a shopper helping himself from a supermarket freezer, the Professor extracts from the body the wind pipe, the thyroid gland, and the oesophagus, each of which is examined visually, weighed and set aside for the lab. "Now the heart" he says, preparing to dive in again, then "Hang on, what's this?" The Professor stops and asked the assistant to look. "I just nudged the lung, see?" he pokes at one of the lungs again. The assistant nods his understanding. "Ask Gabby to come in would you?" the Professor says to him.

"Gabriella Hopkins is another pathologist. My Dad really rates her." Ben leans across to explain to Priya while they wait, both wondering what is concerning Ben's father.

"Sorry guys." the Professor addresses them, scratching his head in puzzlement, "Something really doesn't add up here."

"Professor?" A young woman with large green eyes, oak-coloured skin contrasting with the whiteness of her overall, over which she has placed a white apron, and curly dark hair peaking out from under her cap, raises her eyebrows in a question as she enters the room.

"Thanks for coming, Gabby. I'd appreciate another view. Tell me what you think of these lungs, I've left them in situ." Professor Cohen replies.

Priya watches as the young woman bends over the body on the opposite side to the Professor and looks carefully, her hands behind her back to avoid the temptation to touch before studying ('That could be me one day', Priya thinks).

"Hmmn. You're thinking fluid?" she looks up at Professor Cohen.

"Mmmn" he agrees.

"Have you tried lifting them?" she asks.

"I was going to, once I'd got the heart out, but when I brushed against them I noticed- see what you think." The Professor is careful not to say too much.

Gabriella brings her gloved hands round from behind her to touch the lungs.

"I think you may be right. Weighing will give an indication of course and then the histology will confirm." she asserts.

"Okay." the Professor says firmly, starting to remove his gloves.

Suddenly the tone of the proceedings is changing.

"Ben and Priya, I'm sorry, but you'll have to go." the Professor says, "I was told this was a straightforward overdose but there's more to it and the police will have to scale-up their investigation. Martin, please put him back in the freezer and call Sergeant Griffiths. Gabriella will you assist me please when the police come?" says the Professor as he takes charge of the new situation.

So Priya's first experience of a post-mortem comes to a premature end. She and Ben leave their viewing point reluctantly and divert themselves to the Costa café in the

Infirmary to speculate and compare their reactions. Priya opts for tea, Ben chooses a latte which is prepared by the assistant behind the counter; much better than coffee from the machines which he knows from experience makes it hard to tell what type of coffee it is.

Sitting down, Ben gives a low whistle and flicks his fringe, "The Psalmist was right," he says, "*Man is like a breath; his days are like a passing shadow.*"

"Too right." Priya agrees, then, after a pause, she asks," What was concerning your father?"

"Well." Ben replies, flicking his fringe again as he recalls what his father had said, "When Dad and I spoke it was a straightforward suicide as far as the police were concerned. He was found in the National Space Centre when they opened up yesterday – admittedly a bit unusual - but there were all the signs and paraphernalia around him to suggest a heroin overdose. There's more contaminated heroin coming here through Africa now, it funds terrorist groups you know." Ben adds as an afterthought.

Priya nods her understanding.

Then Ben tells her, "Dad was thinking the toxicology tests – hair and blood - would establish it was heroin. Open and shut case."

"But now it looks suspicious? And the police don't even know who he is?" Priya is intrigued, and thinks that Rita, when she skypes her, will be too.

"Yeah. It seems he wasn't on the staff or anything, just a visitor - and no one has claimed him so far, if you see what I mean." Ben tells her.

"Mmmn." Priya mumbles between sips of her drink; she is wondering why a person would take drugs at the Space Centre.

"And where exactly in the Space Centre did your Dad say he was?" she wants to be reminded.

"It's a long time since I went there, but I think Dad said

something about – what was it - the Mercury Capsule?" he pulls his phone out of his pocket, flicking his fringe as he speaks. "Do you know it at all? Maybe we can find out more online." he adds and scrolls through his phone to find the website for the National Space Centre. The website tells him the Centre was built when he and Priya were five years old (appropriately, in 2001), its presence in the City is a reflection of the involvement of Leicester University in space research. It is sited in the Abbey Meadows area, a few miles out of the City, and its Rocket Tower reaches 42 meters into the sky, making a distinctive landmark.

"I've never been there." says Priya "But I know someone who goes frequently." she adds, thinking of the younger brother of her friend, Rita; Nayan is interested in space exploration and has an annual pass to the Centre, Priya knows.

"So he stopped the PM because of the state of the lungs? They had fluid in them?" is her next question to Ben to check she understands what has happened.

"Seemed so." Ben agrees, swirling the brown liquid of his latte round in his mug. "They will have a good look under the microscope. He wasn't happy with other aspects either was he?" he adds, "The bruising and the burn marks? Sounds like someone had a go at our bloke."

"So your father thinks foul play?" Priya prompts her companion.

"Well, not necessarily." Ben is cautious. "Dad has to be careful if the death looks suspicious. So once he had evidence it was not a clear-cut overdose he had to tell the police." Ben finishes his coffee.

"It's for them and the CPS to decide if anyone else was involved and whether to arrest and charge anyone." he continues.

"Yeah, I get that." Priya acknowledges. "So the lungs might suggest what? Drowning?" she asks incredulously.

"Maybe." Ben replies, inclining his head from side to side as if weighing the idea.

"You don't get water - or whatever - in your lungs and then wander into the Space Centre and kill yourself, do you? It suggests the man was taken to his place of rest by someone else? Dad will get the facts and the police will have to sort it out." he summarises.

"I guess." says Priya, still trying to get her head round it. 'What could have happened to the poor chap?' she thinks.

The thoughts of the two are disturbed by the ringtone on Ben's phone and he leaps up and steps out into the corridor to answer it, seeing the call is from his father.

"Bad luck we couldn't stay for the whole PM." Ben ventures when he returns.

"Epic fail!" Priya agrees as she and Ben commiserate together again.

"That was Dad on the phone. It sounds like it's getting really interesting. I'll have a go at him about us watching another." Ben offers.

Priya nods in thanks. "What was your father's news?" she asks.

"In the PM, as my father suspected, they found water – tap water- in the man's lungs. Together with the burn marks, which they think were caused by a cigarette, it is looking as if someone was responsible for the unknown man's death." he tells Priya, passing his hand through his fringe and making it stick up before he absent -mindedly smooths it down again, all signs his brain is working hard.

Priya waits to hear what more Ben's father may have told him.

"So there is more than a chance that the heroin found near the body was administered by someone else," Ben continues, "That he did not cause his own death. Toxicology results are awaited to confirm whether he was a regular drug user – but there were no signs of it on his body as you know - and whether it was in fact heroin in his system, as the evidence of the syringe and powder round him suggested." Ben pauses to put on his jacket as he prepares to leave the Infirmary.

"Meanwhile," Ben finishes what he has to say, "the police have closed off the Space Centre and are treating it as a crime scene. They will be appealing for witnesses and for anyone who can identify the mystery man."

Chapter

2

"It suddenly struck me that that tiny pea, pretty and blue, was the Earth. I put up my thumb and shut one eye, and my thumb blotted out the planet Earth. I didn't feel like a giant. I felt very, very small."

Neil Armstrong

Thursday, 3rd July 2014 11.30am

"Nayan, it's Zeedan calling. Nayan, it's Zeedan calling." Nayan Patel is in his bedroom at 10 Elm Drive, Oadby, in Leicester, where he lives with his parents and older brother and sister; he has programmed his phone to say who is calling him and the sound pierces his slumber at 11.30am. Nayan opens his eyes slowly, blinking in the grey light created by the dark blue blind at his bedroom window, and shakes his head on the pillow, his unruly dark hair spreading out on the blue pillow case like the tentacles of a large spider.

Nayan's bedroom is at the back of the house. His sister Rita has a room at the front, overlooking the road; she is in there currently, looking at her wardrobe and cosmetics and thinking about what to wear for her school prom next week. Rita's task is interrupted and she is brought to look out of the window, where there are pink blinds to match her décor, by a rattling noise which had crescendoed as it approached the house and ended with a clattering like the sound of a metal tray being dropped from a height. Standing by the lamp post situated directly outside the house, Rita can see a boy of similar stature and appearance to Nayan's. He wears grey jeans with rips at the knees and a t-shirt with a picture of a penguin on it. The boy has positioned his skateboard –

the origin of the noise - against the post and has his phone pressed to his head; he has earphones dangling from the pocket of his jeans.

A moment later Nayan erupts from his room in a cloud of Lynx and energy, runs heavily down the spiral staircase, jumps the last two steps and slams the front door behind him, appearing at the lamp post, with his own skateboard under his arm, to fist bump the other boy. Rita watches as they mount their boards and set off round the corner into Beech Grove, the noise doubled but receding.

"Was that Nayan going out?" Rita hears her mother say downstairs.

Thursday, 3rd July 2014 1.30pm

Nayan and his friends pause to take a selfie in front of the 54 bus before boarding it. Adorned in yellow with pictures of flying saucers on it to advertise the service, the bus takes Nayan and Zeedan, together with Mo and Ricki, school friends they had met in Leicester's town centre, to a cross roads near to the Space Centre, from where they propel their boards along the pavement. There are lockers at the Centre where they plan to store the skateboards when they arrive. As they leave Exploration Drive for the car park and path to the attraction, a surprising sight greets the boys. Figures clad head to toe in white are shuffling into the building through the hatch - like entrance doors, pausing in the doorway to don covers for their shoes. Can this be a space exercise, some holiday entertainment put on by the staff? they think or is it a re-enactment of a scene from a sci-fi book or film perhaps? The boys are aware that the actor Warwick Davies has visited the Centre, for example, when a Star Wars film was showing and people often dress up as their favourite characters. Perhaps this is one of those events?

The police crime scene tape which snakes around the

perimeter of the car park gives the lie to those ideas. These are scene of crime officers, but what crime could have occurred in the alternative universe of the Space Centre to require this level of attention? Nayan wonders.

"Sorry sir." the policewoman is very polite. "It's a crime scene. We can't let anyone in."

The boys shrug exasperatedly and put their hands in their pockets to watch what is happening.

"How long will it take?" Nayan asks, hoping they might have arrived at the end of an investigation and that the tape will soon be removed. He had seen this once before, when a suspicious package turned up in the Haymarket shopping centre but was cleared of anything sinister almost as soon as the police had put up the crime scene tape and started to disperse the crowd.

"I think we'll be here most of the day. Sorry for your disappointment. There are members of staff over there if you want to speak to them." She gesticulates in the direction of a group of red t-shirted young men and women. Some are taking the opportunity to smoke, others are making calls or scrolling through their phones, either leaving news of the disruption or seeking confirmation and explanation from social media sites about what is going on. Nayan edges closer to them to see if he can glean any information.

"So it's about that guy, the one they found in the Mercury Capsule?"

"I think so."

"I thought he killed himself?"

"Wish they'd make their minds up."

"I want to go back in, it's boring out here."

"Where's Jackie? She could tell us to go home!"

"The police may want to question us."

"Oh great! It's all down to Security if you ask me, we didn't see the guy."

The exchanges leave Nayan only slightly more enlightened.

His attention wanders to other bystanders. There are some boys of a similar age to themselves, who are sitting on BMX bikes, or doing wheelies in the car park, and there are families with young children who point at the white suited figures excitedly as if they have dressed up for their benefit. There is a group of bikers with their bikes propped up by the crime scene tape; Nayan can see an England flag – a red cross on a white background - on the back of one of the motorbikes. The riders wear black t-shirts and jeans, heavy boots that look as if they could survive a walk on the moon, and leather jackets or long coats. Also staring at the Centre are some older couples whose disappointed faces suggest it was the destination of choice today. In addition, there are two middle aged men in jeans walking a large Alsatian dog on a short lead, presumably they were passing by and are now curious about the activity at the Centre.

Thursday, 3rd July 2014 10pm

"OMG!" is Rita's reaction that evening on Facetime when Priya contacts her to tell her to watch the local evening news. "There's an item on it – it's an appeal for help to identify a man; but the thing is, Rita, what the police don't say, is that he's dead. I know because I went to his post-mortem! Ben arranged it!"

"That explains it." Rita then says, indignantly.

"Explains what?" Priya looks surprised.

"Why Nayan came back from the Space Centre today in such a bad mood." Rita shakes her head as if this is news Priya should know.

"He did?" Rita notices Priya reach for her comb to pass through her long dark hair while her friend explains.

"He wanted to go there with his mates. They are fellow geeks from the Science Club at school. He got all the way there on the bus-" Rita is waving her hands about airily as she speaks.

"It's the number 54 bus from outside Primark isn't it?" Priya interrupts, showing off knowledge Ben gathered when he looked up the Centre's website.

"That's right," Rita nods. "Across town from the temple. Past Abbey Park. Anyway, they got to the car park and before they could get to the Centre a police officer walked up and stopped them! She said it was closed while they conducted investigations."

"What did Nayan do?" Priya wants to know.

"They went to the industrial museum, it's next to the Space Centre, in the old Abbey Pumping House. Some consolation, but it wasn't the same, though." Priya thinks Rita almost manages to sound regretful on her younger brother's behalf.

"Disappointing." Priya agrees. "You really should see the police appeal. It's Sergeant Griffiths doing it!"

Rita reaches across her bed for the TV remote and searches through the programmes until she finds the news. Soon the Midlands news section starts and Rita watches as the police appeal for help in identifying a man whose picture they show in the form of sketches. The spokesman is Sergeant Griffiths of the Leicester police. Priya and Rita had met the Sergeant some months ago when Rita's older brother, Mohal, found himself in trouble and wrongly accused of murder. Sergeant Griffiths had been one of the officers who had searched Rita's house and Priya had been there at the time. Rita recalls that the rather large figure of Sergeant Griffiths had seemed kindly. On the TV appeal he asks, in his rolling Welsh tones, for anyone who knows the man, or has any information, to come forward. There is a police sketch of a black man in his late twenties. He is drawn bareheaded with short black hair, and also, in another sketch, with a cap and a stud in one ear.

"And that's the chap from the post-mortem you went to?" Rita checks when the item has finished. Priya confirms "Uhhuh."

"Strange they didn't say he was dead." Rita observes, tucking her unruly brown curly hair behind her ear.

"Mmmn. They just said that they wanted to know who he is." agrees Priya.

"And they didn't say where he was found." Rita adds, "The police are being very cagey." she says.

"But fancy you seeing his body!" Rita's tone betrays her envy of her friend.

"There were no identifying marks." Priya tells Rita "There were no tattoos or anything to distinguish him."

"And no possessions on him, no wallet, no watch, no phone?" Rita checks.

"The police certainly didn't seem to have anything to go on according to Ben." Priya confirms.

('Ben again!' thinks Rita, 'He's all she talks about!')

"What about dental records?" is Rita's next suggestion. Her parents run a dental surgery so she is aware that the police use these records in their inquiries

"They've circulated the details. I guess it depends whether he's had any dental work done recently, or in the area. After all he might not even have lived in Leicester!" Priya points out.

"Someone must know him and what happened." Rita adds as they sign off.

Chapter

3

"The scenery was very beautiful. But I did not see The Great Wall [of China]."

> Yang Liwei, China's first
> astronaut (taikonaut)
> speaking in October 2003.

Saturday, 5th July 2014 9am

Two days later, and Rita is again in her bedroom at the front of her parents' house in Elm Drive. She is lying on her pink duvet cover looking round her. Suddenly it feels to her like the room belongs to someone else; to a younger self, not to the Rita of 2014 about to go to uni! She has already made a list of what she wants to take with her when she goes away. If all goes well she will be in uni accommodation for the first term so there is no need to look for places to rent yet.

"Don't take too much." older friends have urged. "You can get most stuff when you're there, when you know what you need."

"Your mother will try to weigh you down with stuff." another said, "but resist!"

"Do take up any offers of bedding." another told her "Quilts and stuff are so expensive. Just ignore the cookery books – you can get what you need online."

Now Rita wonders if her parents will mind if she redecorates her room. ("Just before uni? You're going away anyway!" she imagines the conversation in her head.) There is also a sulky-faced Nayan in her mind ("But I should have her room if she's going away! I'm the only one without an ensuite!").

'Maybe she could offer to do something neutral, something Nayan can live with when she's gone? Maybe she can find a colour scheme she likes that will look ok with his Star Wars posters perhaps?' she thinks. Rita picks up her iPad to look up paint colours, but before she gets far her phone rings. It is Priya on her way to Birmingham for a shopping trip with her sister, Meera.

("I don't know why she wants to go over there." said Priya's father, "What's wrong with the shops in Leicester?"

"They haven't got Selfridges." Priya patiently explained to her father.)

As Meera drives along the motorway, Priya confirms on the phone to Rita that according to Ben there has been no positive response to the police appeal so far. The dead man remains unidentified. The girls sign off and Rita takes up her iPad to look at more makeover ideas.

***

Meera had collected Priya from their parents' house in her Mini car ("I don't know how you can still get behind the wheel" her mother says.) Meera, who married Jai, a University lecturer, two years ago, is over 7 months pregnant, her waist has disappeared and she seems to Priya to be getting larger by the day. She wants to find some comfortable but fashionable clothes to wear ("I'm not being funny but the clothes you sell are too old fashioned for me," she tells her mother.) Meera thinks she might pick up some pretty baby clothes if they see any, but more than anything what she wants is a 'girly' day out with her sister before the impending infant puts paid to all that for a while.

"Let's get our nails done." Meera suggests to Priya as she heads for the M6 which will lead them to the city centre via the A38, the view of the Warwickshire fields giving way to the industrial heritage of Birmingham which is apparent from the raised motorway routes wrapping themselves round the centre of the city like weeds round the stem of a plant.

Alongside the route they see the red brick remnants of factories and warehouses, now being regenerated, and they pass the looming red-brown façade of Fort Dunlop, once the largest factory in the world and now serving as a hotel, and a site for offices and shops. The large RAC control centre, which also borders the motorway, by contrast is made of grey steel and glass and it, like the retail and leisure parks they can see in the middle distance, is picked out in many lights, like a permanent festival decoration.

Parking a few streets from the Bull Ring Centre, it soon becomes obvious that, on yet another warm summer's day, the city centre is very busy and that Meera's extra girth is affecting her speed and mobility in crowds. After getting a manicure, enjoying the rest and the pampering, and taking a selfie in Selfridges, the sisters gather some items from the food hall and graduate along Waterloo Street to seek some peace over a drink in the Museum and Art Gallery café, which Priya had discovered on a previous visit with Rita, thanks to the latter's interest in history.

Priya walks on the outside of the pavement, wearing a green sleeveless shirt with brown cropped trousers and white canvass baseball lace-ups, her dark straight hair swinging in a ponytail tied high on her head as she has seen in a fashion magazine. She carries the shopping to free up her sister to manage her balance better on the irregularly paved footway; Meera wears an oversize pink top above black leggings and wedge heeled sandals; she sports large round sunglasses pushed on to the top of her head of thick dark brown hair which spills out over her shoulders. Even in sandals her feet and ankles feel hot and ungainly and she is finding the irregular pavement surface a trial.

As they reach the neoclassical magnificence of the museum and art gallery, Priya realises she had forgotten there were fairly steep steps up to the entrance and then again inside to the floor where the café is situated but Meera stoutly refuses to look for a lift ("I'm not past it yet!") and struggles upwards resolutely. They turn right at the top of the stairs, pausing at the Museum shop to glance at the necklaces and pictures, diaries and paperweights on offer before walking past what seems to be a miscellany of items including a Pugin rood screen, which Rita had pointed out to Priya on a previous visit, and items of pottery, then through the Buddah room where there are statues of the Buddah and also of Hindu gods, some in wood, some in golden metal, and so, eventually, feeling more relaxed and having got their breath back after the stairs, they make it to the Edwardian tea rooms.

The café is lavishly decorated in shades of orange and green with a mosaic tiled floor and soaring decorated ceiling. The counter is a modern brown and cream counterpart to the historic shell in which it finds itself but fits well with the 'mad hatter' like furniture scattered in a mixture of styles around the café area; there are soft and hard chairs, sofas and cushions interspersed with dining tables and low coffee tables. Unusual shaped lamps add to the eccentric nature of the design.

The sisters choose a soft drink each and a slice of carrot cake to share and rest thankfully on the padded tangerine sofa in the corner from where they can watch other visitors collect their refreshments on the grey trays and discuss the exhibits in the museum and gallery. Priya would like to spend time looking at the Pre-Raphaelite paintings of which the gallery has many examples but Meera is keen to walk up to Harvey Nichols at the Mail Box ("Are you sure you can make it?" Priya checks).

Refreshed by the rest and the tea, they exit to the square where Priya, about to descend the steps, stops suddenly, almost causing Meera, who is a few feet behind, to bump into her. Below them in the square is a busker. The man is playing a trumpet. Greensleeves has just ended and he is starting on a version of Scarborough Fair. A few coins decorate the soft peaked cap he has placed on the ground before him. 'Nothing odd in that' thinks Meera, wondering why her sister has stopped so suddenly.

Priya opens her jaw and closes it several times but no sound emerges. "What's the matter with you?" Meera wants to know, standing alongside her sister.

"That busker," says Priya,"Playing down there, I've seen him before."

"Well?" Meera is impatient. Buskers are everywhere these days she thinks. She looks again at this one, a black man, probably in his late twenties or early thirties. He looks reasonably well dressed, she decides; maybe he is a little thin but he doesn't look as if he needs to beg.

"Oh come on," Meera urges and pulls on her sister's arm, shaking some of the shopping bags in the process. Priya wakes as if from a dream.

"In a moment," she says, removing her phone from her pocket and taking a picture of the trumpet player to Instagram to Rita. The musician looks exactly like the man she had seen with Ben, two days ago, lying dead on the post-mortem table.

Chapter

4

"I think humans will reach Mars, and I would like to see it happen in my lifetime."

Buzz Aldrin

Thursday, 10th July 2014 10pm

A few days later and Rita, Priya and Ben are together in the darkness, lit only by an occasional spotlight which swirls around them; they are turning in circles and spinning around each other on the dance floor like planets whirling in space. Other dancers move swiftly by them like asteroids, narrowly avoiding a collision. Priya shouts "OMG, I can hardly hear you!" Above the cacophony of her Year 13 contemporaries dancing wildly and singing the words of a Rihanna song. She is addressing Rita who is replying to Priya's question "Will you come to Birmingham with me?"

For the Prom the hall of their school in Oadby, Leicester, has been decorated this evening as if for an Oscar party, with gold and silver balloons arched across the ceiling and in doorways, gold foil versions of Oscar statuettes cut out and stuck on the walls, and a red carpet of paper which runs from the school entrance to the hall. Everywhere, couples and groups cluster to take photos or photobomb the pictures of others. Most of the boys are in suits or dinner jackets with black bow ties, like Ben's or looking like prototype versions of James Bond. Some wear coloured bow ties, some have thin strips of coloured material as ties and others have black laces, like strings of liquorice, at their necks; some ties are tied, some are hanging loose around their shirt fronts. Other boys favour no tie and sport high-collared, neru style jackets.

All have paid special attention to their hair, some slicking back their locks with gel and hair spray (Ben has just given his a good comb through), so that most of the boys are unrecognisable from their school day personas as sweatshirt inhabiting, beings with unruly hair. In their Prom outfits the boys give hints of the mature adults they will eventually become.

The girls have also made great efforts with their attire. Their dresses are mostly block colours of blue, red, yellow, or green, in various shades and lengths. Some are knee-revealing, bare-armed and highlighting their chest areas, others are more demure along Catherine Middleton lines. The shiny materials sparkle in the light of the glitter balls installed in the school hall ceiling. Silver and gold shoes are favoured, mostly vertiginously heeled. The Hollywood starlet theme is not universal among the costumes, however, as many female 6th formers are in versions of ethnic dress, with brightly coloured scarves, exotic hats, shimmeringly decorated saris and shalwar kamiz, some with long style tunics and loose fitting trousers, others favouring leg-hugging churidars.

Priya is clad in a soft pale yellow sari, which she carries off elegantly, her many bracelets clinking together as she dances in her silver sandals, her long dark hair combed glossily and woven into a plait which coils over her right shoulder. Priya is pleased to be in low heeled shoes as some of their friends, suffering already, have taken their shoes off and are cradling them in their arms as if they were cherished pets. Priya smiles at her best friend, Rita, who wears a shalwar kamiz in her favourite colour (deep turquoise). She has rows of golden necklaces which accentuate the warm brown of her eyes and has piled her straggly brown hair into a neat knot on top of her head.

As Priya speaks, Ben, her partner for the evening, flicks his fringe and shows off some Jewish dancing steps, his knees bending and straightening exaggeratedly, his arms waving, his fingers occasionally brushing against Priya's. They smile shyly at one another. Another couple whirl by, narrowly avoiding the three of them; they are a dark haired girl in a black lace dress, laughing, and a breathless tall boy in a dark suit with a red cummerband at his waist. Rita had arrived at the prom with them – Abbie and Jack - together with Rohan, who is now standing with a group of his friends, most of the school first XI cricket team, across the room by the chocolate fountain. Rita's brother, Mohal, back from his uni in Hertfordshire, had acted as chauffeur for the four of them and will collect them in the Peugeot later. Priya's brother in law, Jai, had volunteered to collect her from the Prom and take her back with him to her home to Loughborough, as he is in the city centre for a University dinner that evening ("I don't like him leaving Meera alone now she is so pregnant" Priya's mother complained).

Other pupils had made some spectacular entrances to the ball, their families having gone to considerable lengths to make the occasion of their offspring leaving school special, hiring limousines and American style cars to convey them to the Prom, even a 12 seater stretch Humvee from which pupils had spilled, giggling, at the start of the evening. Alcohol is available at the Prom but limited to three drinks each, policed with ultraviolet markings on the back of the hands. As a result, 'preloading' has been popular and several pupils are the worse for wear already. Those, like Priya, Ben and Rita who do not want alcohol, find themselves under pressure to collect drinks for those with stronger tastes, so there is drunkenness, as the head teacher fears every year, but the overall amount of alcohol available is controlled. Two male members of staff act as door staff and search bags for booze; the pupils are wise to this and drink what they have brought outside and out of view,if they can, defying school authority to the last moment.

As the song ends and the music switches to a drum beat, Priya manages to continue the previous conversation by shouting into Rita's ear, "So will you come to Birmingham with me? See if we can spot him?" She is gratified when Rita, who is glancing over the crowd of swaying bodies, thinking there are people here whom she has seen for the last seven years yet who, after today, she may never see again, nods absentmindedly. Priya notices her friend's distant expression and glances at Ben, putting away thoughts of the mystery man on the mortuary table and his likeness to the busker in Birmingham and thinking instead of the shy way that Ben, a few minutes earlier, had taken her arm, covered by the flimsy, flowing material of her sari, and led her out to the dance area.

"Did you see the selfie from space?" Ben Cohen is whispering into Priya's ear now to make sure she can hear in the surrounding noise. Earlier in the week, to mark the Space Centre's 13th anniversary, the Centre had sent its mascot (2.0, two-point-oh) into orbit to get an 'out-of-this-world selfie'. The mini explorer had climbed almost 21 miles – 3 times the altitude of a commercial jet - thanks to a weather balloon. A video camera had recorded the 2 hour journey and the moment 2.0 came hurtling back to earth, landing in a field south of the village of Husbands Bosworth.

"It was well cool!" Ben laughs, "Especially when it landed!" and Priya laughs too.

Now Priya spins around with Ben, throwing back her head. Priya tries to show Ben some Bollywood moves, recalling her friends who had danced in Leicester Cathedral for the Easter service which was televised; she had seen parts of their performance on YouTube. Like them, Priya is moving gracefully with her arms swaying in the air, the green varnish on her nails adding to the effect which makes her arms look like the branches of a tree caught by a breeze. Priya beckons to Rita who joins in the twirling and whirling, swaying and waving her arms with her friends.

Chapter

5

"I can remember in early elementary school when the Russians launched the first satellite. There was still so much unknown about space. People thought Mars was probably populated."

Christa McAuliffe (1948-1986)

Saturday, 12th July 2014 11am

Priya asks "So what are we going to do if we see him?" Although she has instigated this journey to Birmingham with Rita, she is unsure about it now. Rita is behind the wheel of Mohal's Peugeot which their parents have insured for her to drive ("There's no point you having your own car as you'll soon be at uni.")

"We'll look for him in the square and around the centre. If we see him we'll give him some money and get him talking." Priya hears Rita assert confidently. The girls have brought a copy of the Leicester Mercury, the local paper, with them. This has the police sketches in it and a short piece appealing for information. Poor man! Priya thinks as Rita drives along the motorway. He must be stuck in the mortuary; until relatives claim him, how can there be a funeral? And the police need to establish what happened to him.

"What does the pathologist think?" Rita asks as she changes lanes. Priya tells her friend that her phone calls and Facetime chats with Ben have yielded the information that the man's lungs had water in them, suggesting drowning, but not in quantities expected if a person is fully emersed in water for any length of time.

"So." Priya recounts to Rita what Ben had told her, "The

police are working on the theory that either he was plunged into water, say in a basin, or, looking at the state of his lungs and airway, that water was dripped on him."

"Waterboarding you mean?" Rita asks Priya, surprising her friend with how quickly she can leap to a conclusion it had taken time for Priya to reach.

"Well yes, it seems a possibility." Priya tells her friend, nodding. "It was tap water, Leicester's finest, so not from a river or, God forbid, a lavatory. Put it together with the recent burn marks and it starts to look…"

Before she can finish, Rita's quick mind has helped her interrupt; still looking at the road ahead she says "Like he was tortured? Grim! But whatever for? Why would anyone do that?"

"Ben says the police are keen to find out. What information did he have and who wanted it? Could be to do with anything, but the people who questioned him must have been desperate." Priya thinks out loud.

"Hmmn." Rita seems to be considering the possibilities, then she says "And why was he in the Space Centre? He didn't work there?"

"Ben says the police have no idea. He wasn't on the payroll or known to any of the staff, although they are being fairly tightlipped apparently; according to what Ben's father can gather, no one can explain how this happened and why he wasn't discovered until they opened the Centre the next day." Priya tells her friend recounting a recent skype conversation with Ben.

"Nayan was well fed up the Space Centre was closed when he went, the day you went to the postmortem. He's going back with his friends to make up for it!" Rita says, looking across at her friend.

Priya is concerned that thinking about the mystery will distract Rita from driving, so she decides to ask Rita a question on history, her favourite topic.

"How did Birmingham get its name anyway? It's so different from Leicester." she asks.

"Random!" Rita expostulates, "It's from a chap called Peter de Birmingham!"

"No way!" laughs Priyah. It was not what she had imagined.

"Yeh. Basically, he applied in the 12th century for a licence for a market and Birmingham really took off from there. First there was trade and later, of course, the City was a major player in the industrial revolution. Matthew Boulton and Soho House were instrumental in the development of science and engineering and Birmingham was well placed with the potteries around; that's why they built the canal network."

"Like in Brindley Place?" Priya asks, remembering her walk alongside the canalside there with her sister. "I like it there."

"Yeah. That's one of the many parts of the canal system." Rita tells her. "There's an exhibition about the history of the City in the Museum and Art Gallery if you want to know more."

"Hmmn." Priya's not so sure she wants to go to an exhibition when she can get what she needs from Rita.

"So it's not as old as Leicester, then?" she asks, "We had Vikings and Romans and all sorts didn't we?"

"That's right," says Rita, checking in her rear-view and wing mirrors in order to pull into the left-hand lane "I expect there was a small settlement here but it was nothing like as important as Leicester until Peter de Birmingham and his market."

"What did the Romans call Leicester?" Priya follows a train of thought while wishing she had not put her hair in a plait as she would like to put a comb through it, but undoing the plait would be a lot of work.

"Ratae Corieltauvorum." Rita tells her confidently.

"Because of the Corieltauvians, a Celtic tribe. It used to be thought it was Ratae Coritanorum but that seems to have been a mistake. Ratae means ramparts. There's lots of info about it at the Jewry Wall Museum of course."

"Oh yes," Priya says, "That's another thing. I've always wondered why the museum is called that. Is it to do with Jewish people?" she asks.

Rita thinks of Ben, Priya's 'friend', and wonders if that has prompted the idea.

"No, I don't think so, but to be honest I don't know much about Jewish people in Leicester." Rita glances across at her friend, "Maybe I'll find out for you before we go to uni!" she offers.

That turns Priya's mind to another subject. "Aren't you worrying about your A-level results?" she asks her friend.

"Oh no" Rita replies, "I've better things to think about!"

"What things?" asks Priya, who is curious as she spends a lot of her time worrying that she won't get the grades she needs to get to Oxford, or to be a doctor at all.

"Well, Richard III and the Wars of the Roses for sure." Rita, who has an offer from Warwick University to study history, replies, surprisingly. Priya knows her friend loves history, but this is taking her obsession to a new level!

"I'm going to the new visitor centre when it opens" Rita tells her, "Oh, by the way, you remember my project on Magna Carta?"

Priya nods slowly (does she?- she is not sure).

Rita continues "Have you seen they are going to create a Magna Carta trail?" she asks. Not surprisingly, Priya shakes her head. It has not been one of her preoccupations.

"What is it?" she queries.

"It will show the routes associated with the Charter. The Battlefields Trust are organising it. I saw on the net. One trail will go from London to Runnymede."

"Where it was signed?" says Priya.

"Sealed." corrects Rita.

"Another will go from Salisbury." Rita goes on.

"You went there didn't you?" Priya interrupts, recalling now some of the things Rita had told her about the Charter.

"Yeh. It will go from Salisbury to the West Country. Another will include St Albans." Rita tells her more.

"You've been there too." says Priya, thinking her friend has practically done the trail before it has been created.

"…and Bury St Edmunds where a group of barons met and swore an oath to compel John to accept the Charter of Liberties which came before the Great Charter. The Battlefield Trust are keen it is not seen just as an historical event but as the start of democracy and the beginning of the rule of law. It's very exciting!"

Priya smiles at her friend's enthusiasm.

Rita drives on. As they approach the junction for the centre of Birmingham she says "Oh. And I'm thinking of redecorating my room, want to help?"

The traffic gets busy after that so Priya cannot ask more. Approaching the city centre, Rita steers for a car park and follows a queue of vehicles up the ramped entrance. Taylor Swift is playing on her iPhone which is plugged into the car and the two girls sway in time to the beat as they wait their turn to park. Priya is impressed with Rita's confidence behind the wheel, she has more courage than her own sister who had cautiously parked a few streets from Birmingham's centre on their visit, not wishing to tangle with too much urban traffic ("Before you know it, you're off on one of those motorways that snake around the town and you can't get back to the centre." had been her voiced fear.)

Walking through the streets near New Street Station, Priya notices how much construction work is involved in the station facelift; the pavements are disrupted by temporary barriers and it is hard for the young women to keep a sense of direction. Lines of people walk on the permitted routes like rows of ants. The friends pass two white female Jehovah's Witnesses with a portable stand containing copies of their magazine, The Watchtower, warning of impending doom and the importance of God's plan; a group of Asian men is gathered round a table offering guides to the Qu'ran and leaflets asking 'What is the real purpose of my life?'; and a tall black man with a portable megaphone is preaching about the redemptive power of Christ and the need to repent. If the citizens of Birmingham feel they are on the wrong spiritual path there are plenty of people prepared to put them straight, Priya thinks. They pass an older Muslim man wearing a floor length tunic and talking to a youth, "Obedience" he says, "It is all about obedience."

The noise and bustle of Birmingham is similar to that of the girls' hometown. Both have shopping streets teeming with people of many races, colours, creeds and dress. Various tongues pierce the air; rapid, urgent, Eastern European tones, the more subdued, rattling, Asian languages, lilting Caribbean softer tones. The languages are often interspersed with English in words and phrases like 'Awesome!', 'Primark', 'You get me?', 'New Street', 'Waste of space', 'Why I bother'; to anyone not familiar with the language of the speaker, these words appear like clues or signs on a motorway. The English spoken in Birmingham, as Priya noted on her visit with Meera, tends to have a rounded but nasal quality, whereas the Leicester accent sounds harsher, with the ends of words almost unfinished, like a jagged slice of stilton with the blue veins running through it, the edges blurred. The accent is even mocked – or celebrated - in the Leicester Information Centre, Priya and Rita know, where they have laughed together at the mugs bearing the legend 'I luv Lestah!'.

Rita and Priya today wear jeans and both have on their leavers' sweat shirts, as the sun has yet to penetrate the clouds, although it is promised for later; the royal blue tops have the number 14 picked out in white on the back, with the names of each of the leavers written inside the outline of the number. The girls stop at a Caffe Nero on Waterloo Street, having passed Birmingham's Cathedral, a squat Georgian building in the middle of a green area ideal for shoppers to rest, or for office workers to take their lunch on fine days. Contrasting with the smartly dressed people who are today sitting on the benches, their bags circling their legs, lying on the grass there are a few people who look like they live on the streets. The group is gathered by a tree and occasionally one of them hunts for treasure in the bins. A female Big Issue seller with a long brown skirt, a flowing long-sleeved top in a similar shade and a black hijab on her head, stands by the entrance to the path which crosses the grass, smiling endlessly to encourage buyers. The girls collect tea to take away and wander down in the direction of the Museum and Art Gallery and the square where Priya had seen the busker. Rita had agreed from the Instagrammed photo that there was a possible resemblance with the picture the police had circulated.

Around the square are Victorian buildings like tributes to the classical age; pillars, porticoes and stone friezes of a size and grandeur not seen since the Parthenon in Athens or the Pantheon in Rome. Concrete shapes like giant cannon balls lie casually as if abandoned there in front of a building called the Council House. Queen Victoria stands on a plinth at one end, looking down disdainfully on the people who move up and down the steps at the edge of the paved area like figures in an Esher drawing. As the pair approach the square they glance hopefully at one another. It sounds as though their luck is in! The strains of Greensleeves dance on the air above the shoppers going hastily across the path of Priya and Rita,moving to their left towards the retail area or to their right if they are seeking culture, and taking the most direct route to the Gallery or the ICC where the Birmingham Symphony Orchestra have their home.

Priya soon spots the trumpet player, standing by a statue, his cap at his feet. "You see." she hisses although no one would hear her above the hubbub of the people in the square and the sudden rush of a helicopter which chooses that moment to pass overhead.

"See, when he closes his eyes to concentrate on the music, that's when he has the best resemblance to the body I saw." Priya urges her friend to see the similarity.

Rita glances from the newspaper sketch to the musician and back again. She says her friend has a point, but can they be absolutely sure? A lot of people probably look like that. Rita's determination seems to be starting to desert her, but Priya is not to be put off. "Come on!" she says boldly and the two girls descend the steps, Priya in the lead, Rita following, to stand by the man's cap. Rita puts down her tea and searches in her Cath Kidston bag for her purse, unzipping it and flicking through the change to find something suitable to place in the hat.

The man notices them and brings Greensleeves to an end. "You like the music?" he asks in a Birmingham accent (so that 'like' sounds as if there is an 'o' before the 'i').

"Yeah." says Priya finding her courage. "Where did you learn to play?" (Priya doesn't know why she asks that; maybe she thinks it may be useful to gain his confidence?).

"I teach music." was his surprising reply. It explains the get-up thinks Priya - smart trousers and a waist coat, a cut above the usual busker's attire.

"I like" (again, pronounced as 'loike') "to bring" (he pronounces the final 'g') "people pleasure. It gives me a kick, you know? And the money" (he says it like 'munnie') "comes in handy."

"I can imagine," Rita joins in. "This may sound strange but we couldn't help noticing…" and she starts to unfurl the page of the Leicester Mercury with the sketches in it.

"Hey, what's your game?" The man is immediately

suspicious Priya can see. "I don't like" ("loike") this. I'm not doing anything wrong." (hard 'g' again) "You know I've" ("oive") a perfect right to be here."

The man is agitatedly collecting up his hat and the change lying on it.

"No, it's nothing like that…" Priya tries to explain but he has turned away quickly and starts to flee the square, trumpet in one hand, hat in the other.

He mutters something to them as he exits, "Oim out of here." or something similar, and the girls are left to watch his retreating back.

"Shall we follow him?" Priya is not willing to give up now.

"No, that would be crazy, we don't know the town centre as well as he probably does, we'd never keep up with him." Rita retorts, sighing and folding up the newspaper page.

"So now what?" Priya sits down disconsolately on the steps at the edge of the square. Of all the possible scenarios – anger, denial and laughter - this was not one she had imagined or planned for.

Rita puts the newspaper back into her red bag and sits beside her friend, then takes a sip of her tea.

"Well I agree with you there's a resemblance. And that it's weird. He even has an earring in his left lobe, like in the sketch. He must be related to the dead man somehow. A cousin perhaps? And then he was so defensive and anxious. He so didn't want to speak to us! What was that all that about? I think the best we can do," Rita's phone starts to ring before she can finish, "is call Sergeant Griffiths" she adds as she flicks at the screen on her phone to answer the call.

Priya hears Rita ask a few questions of the caller as the friends exchange quizzical looks.

"Well that's weird!" Rita says when the call has ended with her promising to visit the speaker. "You remember Mr Gregson, the man who used to live next door to my family?"

Priya nods. They had visited the elderly man at Oak

Trees, his care home. He had seemed an intelligent and kindly person and had helped Rita with some of her history projects. Why would he be calling Rita? Priya wonders.

"Well a friend of his at the care home has gone missing and he wants my help."

"Missing?" Priya wonders why Mr Gregson thinks Rita can help.

"I said I'd go and see him, you should come too." Rita says, standing up and getting ready to leave. Priya has no time to object.

"Why?" is all that Priya can get in.

Rita's reply causes her surprise "Because the missing old lady recently visited the Space Centre, on the day your mystery man was killed!"

Chapter

6

"I don't know what you could say about a day in which you have seen four beautiful sunsets."

John Glenn

Saturday, 12*th* July 2014 4pm

Priya and Rita find that Mr Gregson is in his room at the care home in Thurmaston when they return to Leicester ("He has not been feeling so well today, I think this business with Mrs Cummings has upset him." the care assistant, wearing a blue tabard over black trousers, her curly blond hair escaping from the scarf tied over the top of her head, tells them.) She knocks on the door and ,on hearing Richard Gregson, she pushes it open and ushers the girls in with a "Cheerioh then" as she leaves them.

"So good of you to come." says Richard Gregson, seated in his wheelchair and looking smart as usual in a blue striped shirt and grey corduroy trousers. Priya looks around his room, thinking if she wants to become a doctor she may step into many rooms arranged like this since older people form the largest percentage of the patient population. His room is immaculately tidy, the books and ornaments on the dark wooden bookshelves, shining and reflecting the afternoon sun, are in regimented order, nothing out of place. Priya notices there are only two photographs, one of a younger Mr Gregson with a black moustache instead of the grey one that covers his top lip now, and one of an elegant lady looking like a 1960s film star; that must be his late wife she thinks. The bed has a green patchwork cover over it and a large pale green rug extends over much of the beige carpet. Gardening books sit on the table and Priya sees that the bay window by which Mr Gregson is sitting gives him a view of the garden at the back of the home, which sprawls below them as they are two flights up. A few people can be seen ambling in the grounds, the sun having come out as promised and provided another warm day.

Priya and Rita seat themselves in the wicker chairs placed either side of the dark wood table.

"I've got these for you!" like a magician, Mr Gregson reaches into a bag under the table and produces with a flourish two cartons of orange juice and a packet of wafer biscuits.

"I got them from the shop here." he chuckles.

"That's very kind." says Priya.

"Thanks" the girls say, helping themselves. Priya thinks that although confined to a wheelchair, Mr Gregson's mental faculties seem as sharp as ever, he has even remembered that these are Rita's favourite biscuits.

"Now tell us what's been going on" Rita urges.

As the girls unwrap the biscuits and Mr Gregson – who declines one ("I have diabetes now, I have to be careful") – tells his story, Priya becomes increasingly concerned. He tells them that a resident, Maureen Cummings, whose room is next to his, could not be found at tea time last Saturday. At first it was assumed she had gone for a walk, but when a search of the grounds produced nothing the staff began to get alarmed. "The police have searched everywhere and put up posters; they've been checking sheds and outhouses or other places she might have gone for shelter" (Mr Gregson's voice trembles as he says this)," as well as checking any woodland or fields within walking distance." he finishes.

"What do her family say? They must be upset?" Priya wants to know.

Mr Gregson says there is one daughter and she lives in Canada. She has young children and can't come over at the moment.

"So she is your friend. Is that why you are concerned?" Priya tries to coax information out of Mr Gregson to see if anything else about the disappearance is troubling him.

Mr Gregson, whose shoulders seem hunched in his chair and whose bushy grey moustache seems to be drooping or wilting with the anxiety, says, "Maureen was upset. It started after some of us went on a trip to the Space Centre. Have you been?" his face brightens and his eyes twinkle as he recalls the visit,

"They have rockets and displays on the history of space exploration and astronauts of the past, it quite took me back. The Sky at Night with Patrick Moore, those moon landings! Such exciting times! It's all commercial now, payloads and sponsors and space tourism, that's the talk these days." he sighs. "Have to move with the times I suppose."

"When was the visit?" Priya checks.

"It was a Tuesday. We always have trips on a Tuesday. The 1st of July." Mr Gregson is clear and the girls exchange a knowing look.

"And Mrs Cummings?" Rita says before she sucks the last of the juice from the carton. Priya thinks Rita is concerned about the time; she needs to take Priya home and then deliver the car back for Mohal to use later.

"Maureen seemed agitated when she got on the mini bus to leave the Space Centre," Mr Gregson says, but he tells the friends that he couldn't speak to her as he was in a special space on the bus allocated for wheelchairs. Later in the day he noticed she barely touched her evening meal ("Which was not like her at all." he tells Rita and Priya) so he had tackled her when they sat together in the residents' lounge after dinner.

"She gets a bit confused, of course," Mr Gregson explains, "dementia is affecting her thinking. Sometimes she'll be right as rain, others she'll struggle for words or phrases. She covers it up pretty well by using bland expressions – 'Oh I expect so' or 'Nothing would surprise me!' which cover most contingencies, but this was something more. She kept saying the aliens had given her a present of the sun." 'I ought to have kept it.' she said, or something like that. She was rocking back and forth. I did mention it to the staff and they said they'd see if she needed a sleeping pill. Maybe she's overdone it, got overexcited on the trip, they said."

Priya stares out of the window, trying not to look Rita. She knows her friend is fond of Mr Gregson but the tale of 'a present of the sun' sounds like the story of a confused old lady.' What can they do to help?' she thinks.

"Anyway, at the weekend I heard some noises from her room, like books being dropped on the floor, then I heard her door close at about two in the afternoon, last Saturday, and that was the last I saw of her." he finishes.

"Has she done this before?" Priya wants to know, thinking that a week is a long time to be missing, she is not hopeful that the woman will be found alive, but she does not want to worry Mr Gregson any more.

"No, I don't think so, it's quite uncharacteristic." the old man tells her.

"How can people just leave the home anyway?" Rita wants to know. "Surely they are locked in for their safety? Sorry Mr Gregson," she adds seeing the look of surprise on his face, "But you know what I mean?" she adds.

"Oh no," Priya explains as this is a question she had looked up on her phone while Rita drove them to Thurmaston; she was curious to know the position. "If people can make their own decisions they can leave if they want to, just like you or me. The Home is not supposed to lock them in. Where people can't make decisions for themselves, and their care is provided by the local authority, the Home needs to comply with the Deprivation of Liberty Safeguards, or 'DOLS' as they are known for short, otherwise it's unlawful to stop the person leaving. There has to be an application, usually by the local authority, to the Court of Protection.So the Home would not have been able to 'lock her in' as you say unless they had applied for permission, which I'm guessing is not the case?" she looks to Mr Gregson for confirmation which he nods to give, "There's quite a backlog of applications according to the care staff" he tells the girls.

"So it's not easy. Most practical arrangements do work though, and aren't challenged, but they do rely on cooperation." Priya finishes.

"Oh, okay, so they couldn't stop her leaving." says Rita sounding impressed by Priya's knowledge.

"What about friends or old work colleagues? People she might have gone to see?" Priya suggests.

Mr Gregson tells them that there are no friends that he knows of ("When you get to our age a lot of them have died." he says mournfully). Then he tells them that Mrs Cummings enjoyed doing crossword puzzles and that in the Second World War she had worked at Bletchley where the code breaking work took place.

"Did the police or staff check her room?" Rita asks "There might be some clues there."

"I don't know," Mr Gregson acknowledges. "But she did leave a clue in my pigeon hole." he adds with a twinkle in his eyes.

The girls both give him in an amazed look. While he has their full attention he pulls from the bag by his chair an envelope and empties the contents onto the table. It is a key and the envelope has a picture drawn on it. The drawing is of a space rocket.

Saturday, 12th July 2014 6pm

"What do you make of it?" Priya asks Rita when they are driving on the A6 to Loughborough to take Priya home. "It's just a coincidence that they visited the Space Centre the same day as the dead man, and that Mrs Cummings got agitated after that, right?" she glances at her friend.

"It may be!" Rita doesn't sound too convinced, "But all the same I think I will mention it to Sergeant Griffiths".

"Are you sure?" Priya is anxious about the reception Rita will get.

Rita has just pulled up outside Priya's house when Priya's phone rings – "It's my Mum, probably wondering where we are-" and at the same time Mrs Shah can be seen opening her front door and rushing out and down the path in front of the semi-detached house to the car. Priya is embarrassed to see her mother is wearing her 'leisure suit' – the purple sweat pants and top she usually wears for relaxing at home, and she has only pink slippers on her feet, which slap against her soles as she runs awkwardly, the door to the house left wide open. Clearly something has happened.

"Oh Priya! Your sister! Oh dear!" the words tumble out breathlessly.

While Rita carefully applies the handbrake and switches off the engine, Mrs Shah continues the conversation with her daughter through the now - open passenger window.

"Meera? Is she ok?" Priya asks, concerned.

"Oh yes, at least I think so, but she's gone into labour! The baby's coming! And it's too early!"

"Oh dear," says Priya. "Where is she? What do the doctors say?"

"Oh doctors!" Mrs Shah's tone is contemptuous, "What do they know? She felt unwell and called Jai who came home and took her to hospital. He phoned me from there about five minutes ago. It sounds like it's all happening very fast."

Priya undoes her seat belt and opens the car door.

"Thanks Rita." she says, "Sounds like I'm needed on baby duty."

"You'll be okay to get to the hospital if you need to?"

Rita asks her. "I can always tell Mohal I need the car for an emergency."

"No, no!" Mrs Shah is shaking her head. "I will drive us, just as soon as we know what is happening." Her phone, which is in her hand, rings.

"Oh dear! Oh dear!" Mrs Shah utters.

Priya turns to shrug at her friend.

"I'll let you know!" she yells as she follows her agitated mother back to the house.

"I'll wait and make a couple of calls." Rita shouts back through the driver's window of the car.

"Come in if you like!" her friend responds, "If you can bear it!" she adds, noticing as she approaches the house the persistent beep of an alarm. Priya is vaguely aware of Rita rushing past her to the kitchen to quell the alarm, but she is preoccupied with trying to overhear her mother's telephone conversation.

Priya and Mrs Shah are oblivious to what Rita is doing in the kitchen as they stand in the living room listening to the voice on the phone which is on loud speaker. "…eclampsia… emergency C section – doing well…"

And then Priya is dancing into the kitchen to join Rita, and takes her friend by both hands to twirl her round, and gallop with her down the hall and back again.

"I'm an aunty! I'm an aunty! She's had the baby!" Priya's plait waves around as she sways her head in her excitement.

"Wow!" says Rita. "That was quick! Boy or girl?"

"It's a boy," Mrs Shah shouts from the living room, asserting proprietary rights over this, her first grandchild, "5 pounds 2 ounces so not bad for 34 weeks! Meera is okay but still woozy from the anaesthetic. Jai has seen him. He looks fine. They're taking him to the special care unit." The information tumbles out of her.

"Your father!" Mrs Shah exclaims. "I must tell your father! He's on his way back from Harrogate. I do hope he gets back soon!"

"Shall I make us some tea?" offers Rita.

Chapter

7

"When I first looked back at the Earth, standing on the Moon, I cried."

Alan Shepard

Sunday, 13th July 2014 1pm

Priya says "We need to go the Infirmary," as she climbs into the Peugeot which is once more outside her house with Rita at the wheel, Mohal having returned the car in the early hours ("You put a lot of miles on that car" their father, Jahi, complains).

"When are visiting hours?" Rita wants to know. "We need to go to the Space Centre too."

Parking in Havelock Street, the girls enter through the automatic doors and, asking after Meera, are directed to the maternity ward. They join groups of families and friends bedecked with teddy bears, cards and balloons making a similar pilgrimage. Priya has brought a small soft blue ball on a ribbon for the new arrival and some chocolates for Meera; her mother had been uncertain whether they would allow any gifts into the neonatal unit but she was sure Meera would appreciate chocolates to cheer her up. They wait to be buzzed into the ward and, when they are admitted, gaze around at the beds, seeking a familiar face in these unfamiliar surroundings. Then they see Meera holding court in the bed by the window or, rather, a weakened version of Priya's sister, who sits propped up against the pillows sipping a glass of water and gesticulating from the elbow down with her free hand like a strange puppet show.

"He's only so big." Meera is explaining to her mother as

the girls approach. She holds her hands apart like a fisherman boasting about a catch.

"But he's a little fighter!" Jai adds, pushing his spectacles back against the bridge of his nose. "He keeps on reaching for the label on his cot, as if he wants to knock it off!"

"Determined, like you Meera." says Mrs Shah who, Rita sees, has a serene glow about her today in contrast to the agitated confusion of the day before.

"Here you are!" she finally notices her other daughter who bends to kiss and congratulate her sister and hands over the toy and the chocolates. "How sweet!" Meera says, then tears start to appear in her eyes, "Oh dear, I can't imagine him being well enough to play with this!" she wails, holding up the ball.

Mrs Shah gives Priya an admonitory look.

"Your father will be back with the tea soon." Jai tries to soothe his wife.

"Why don't I take them over to see the baby? Maybe you can get some rest too?" he ventures.

"Good plan." for once Meera is acquiescent and she slides slightly down the bed as Mrs Shah jumps up with alacrity. "Yes let's go and see him and leave you in peace!" she declares and leads the way out of the ward. Jai bends to kiss his wife and exchange a few words before he follows the women to the lift. Priya notices that all the other mothers on the ward have their babies by their bedside, in transparent cots; it must be hard for Meera not to be with her baby, she thinks.

The Infirmary lives up to its 'Royal' name as a royal theme has invaded the minds of those who named the various parts of it and signs point to Balmoral, Windsor, Osborne and Victoria as they make their way towards a covered pedestrian bridge which links the building to 'Kensington' where Priya sees the neonatal unit is.

"Will they let us all in?" is Mrs Shah's next anxiety, her eagerness to see her first grandchild clear from her intense expression.

"It's probably two at a time." says Jai, "But it can depend who's on duty. One Sister is more relaxed than the other. We'll see."

They cross the bridge, watching others returning from Kensington with mixed emotions on their faces; some look worried, others relieved and relaxed. Several carry toddlers in their arms and Priya thinks how difficult it must be to have a baby who needs extra care if you already have a young family. She watches the doctors, whose ranks she wants to join one day, coming and going in the crowd, easy to spot with stethoscopes round their necks, or iPads on their arms, on which they look at scans, the women in black skirts or trousers and bright shirts, the men in pale coloured shirts and brown or green trousers. They have an easy confident way of walking around this building which is their place of work and more familiar to them than to the visitors.

At the entrance to the neonatal unit they all use the antiseptic gel to wash their hands as requested. Jai gets himself buzzed in with his mother in law while Priya and Rita wait, watching them through the glass in the ward door. Priya sees her mother bend over a cot and can almost hear her delight such is the joyfulness of her body language. Mrs Shah put her hands to her face in pleasure and smiles at Jai. A nurse in a dark blue uniform comes over to talk to them and then, Priya can hardly believe it, she lifts the little bundle out of the cot and hands him to his father! Mrs Shah is practically clapping her hands and doing a dance with excitement. Jai holds his son like he is made of china, scarcely daring to move but, encouraged by the nurse, he takes a few careful steps, with Mrs Shah behind as his acolyte and there he is on the other side of the door, showing off his child to his sister in law and her friend.

"Oh." gasps Priya, "Look at him!"

Priya takes in the wrinkled face and tiny hands which are

all that can be seen of her white clad nephew. On his head the baby wears a yellow knitted hat ("Early babies can have difficulty maintaining their temperature." Mrs Shah explains later on the walk back to see Meera.) and is amazed that something so delicate - looking will, God willing, develop into a full size human being, probably looking not unlike Jai for all Mrs Shah's wishful thinking about "Meera's nose and your father's eyes." The small parcel opens one eye to peer at the world, then opens the other. The eyes are dots which seem to swim around in their cavities, then he blinks and closes them again as if to say "that's enough of the world for now."

Jai and his mother-in-law process back to the cot where he lays his son down reverently, arranging the blanket round him, then he stands back to take a photo (making sure there is no flash to alarm the little one) and he and Mrs Shah exit the unit to rejoin Rita and Priya.

"Isn't he lovely?" Mrs Shah's face is shining and energised with pride, while Jai looks a bit exhausted after the visit. "We'll go and get a cup of tea. Maybe you and Dad could join us?" Priya says tactfully to her mother, thinking that the new parents may appreciate some time to themselves.

"Oh we may." Mrs Shah says airily "But I want to see what your sister thinks about the latest picture. And you haven't told me what you are thinking of for names!" Jai casts a despairing look in Priya's direction which signals 'nice try' then he and his follower turn to the lift to go back to the ward while Rita and Priya head for the Costa Café near the Accident and Emergency Department.

The girls have the café entrance in their sight when to their left a lift door opens – it is one of the wide lifts set aside for hospital trolleys and not for visitor use. A man lies on the trolley, clearly badly injured judging by the number of medical staff around him. One holds a drip, another seems to be checking his pulse.

"Look!" says Priya nudging Rita, "I'm not imagining this am I?"

The girls hear what the doctors are saying as they peer to see better what is happening.

"Michael Simmonds aged 29, stab wound to abdomen, blood loss stemmed at the scene, weapon not found…" intones a paramedic among the crowd round the trolley.

A look of surprise crosses Rita's face when she too realises that the patient pointed out by her friend is the busker, the trumpet player who had run away from them in Birmingham only yesterday! What is he doing in Leicester? And what has happened to him? Priya is thinking.

"…morphine… blood pressure, ….gcs…" the figures roll on while the girls gaze quite inappropriately at the wounded man, the trolley being propelled past them and through a door marked 'Resuscitation'.

"OMG!" Rita says. The girls look at each other's astonished faces and walk like zombies to the café, not discussing what they have seen until they are sitting at one of the plastic tables with a hot chocolate each.

"What do you think's going on?" Priya speaks first.

"I have literally no idea!" says Rita "but unless there are three of them – which is possible but unlikely – the man who is a dead ringer for your guy in the mortuary here, and who we saw in Birmingham, has just turned up in A and E , having been stabbed. You know what would clinch it…" she trails off as they watch another paramedic appear from the lift carrying various possessions, a coat, a pair of shoes, a hat and…

Rita barks a laugh and continues, "Would be if he had his trumpet with him!" She finishes her sentence. There among the possessions which the paramedic is now taking into the Resuscitation room is a shiny silver trumpet, just like the one the friends last saw in the busker's hand as he ran away from them.

"I'm confused." says Priya, "How is he here? Why is he here?"

"I don't know." says Rita "And Sergeant Griffiths is going to get even more fed up with me." she adds as she pulls out her phone.

Sunday, 13th July 2014 3pm

It is a relatively short journey from the Infirmary to the National Space Centre. Driving down Belgrave Road, familiar to the girls for its shops and restaurants and as the site of festivals and processions such as at Divali, Rita and Priya pass near the Shree Siva Muragan Temple at Abbey Mill. Then they turn to go past Abbey Park where there are posters advertising the Dragon Company's outdoor Shakespeare productions this year, which are Twelfth Night and the Merchant of Venice. Rita and Priya know some of the members of the company as the actors used to stay at Athena Maitland's Sundial Bed and Breakfast, where the girls have worked, but fewer of them do now as they associate it with the sad murder of one of their company, a murder which Rita helped to solve.

They turn right at the traffic lights and right again at another set which takes them to Exploration Drive and the generous sized car park for the Space Centre and the Technology Museum. It being the summer school holiday, the car park is over half full. Stepping out of the parked Peugeot and walking to the Centre, Rita and Priya can see above them the notorious tower which stands out on the skyline for several miles and below at their feet are white foot marks laid out like the footsteps of an astronaut; if you step on them, as several young children ahead of the girls are doing, you feel as if your space journey is beginning.

Arriving at the entrance, the girls find the doors are designed like hatches, it is as if you are stepping into a spacecraft. 'No wonder Nayan likes coming here!' Rita thinks. The design inside is industrial, modern, sparse and evocative of the hold of a space ship. Rockets are suspended from the ceiling and technology buzzes and blips at the displays. They queue for their tickets which automatically become annual passes (hence Nayan can afford to return as many times as he wants, Rita learns) and they offer these slender blue cards to a bar code reader to be admitted to the exhibitions through a turnstile. They have tickets for the display in the Planetarium at 4.15 so there is time to look around first.

"What are we looking for?" Priya whispers to her friend.

"Anything the police may have missed!" Rita is optimistic. "After all, this is where it happened, and…" she rummages in her red bag, "I have this!" She produces the key which Mr Gregson had given her.

"How do you know it belongs here?" asks Priya.

"Well, she drew a picture of a rocket on the envelope didn't she?" says Rita "I think that's a clue! It must belong to a locker here!"

Before seeking out the lockers, the girls discover there is a range of exhibits available in the six main galleries of the Centre. They go first to look at the Mercury Capsule on the ground floor, where the body was found. This was part of a USA manned venture into space; they see that the Centre also has one of the few Russian Soyuz craft on show in Western Europe. The Mercury Capsule turns out to be a low grey-coloured vehicle, the interior like that of a narrow boat but with electronics on every wall. It was hard to imagine that any astronaut had lived and worked in this confined space. It was also sad to think that this was where the stranger had died. Any evidence of that event had been removed of course.

There are also displays, which the girls are drawn to, about what people have thought about the universe through the ages and various creation myths from around the world, telling stories of how the universe came into being. Most of the myths begin with the earth as a void and empty or else formed only of water. Eggs feature too, which is an idea that Rita and Priya are familiar with from the Upanishads. The displays tell of a Chinese creation myth of heaven and earth being in chaos like a chicken's egg which was then divided, half of it becoming Yang, the heavens, and the other half Yin, the earth. According to another display, in the Aztec tradition creation began when the Lord/Lady of duality created itself, embodying male and female, good and bad, and gave birth to four other gods who created the world. In the Egyptian tradition there were many stories they learn; one the girls like involves the lifeless watery abyss of chaos and gods formed from the vegetation that grew from the silt including Shu the god of air and Tefnut the goddess of moisture and fertility; some say Shu and Tefnut were created by 'sneezing' and 'spitting', where Shu is the sound of sneezing and Tef the sound of spitting. This makes the girls giggle.

There are displays for each of the planets and quotes from famous physicists like Stephen Hawking. The girls pass explanations about the history of space exploration, and information about various astronauts. Rita can also see the stands that Nayan likes best, the interactive screens where you can test your skills as an astronaut (patience bring one of them, as well as the ability to work in a team; Rita has not observed either quality in her younger brother, she thinks). Michael Collins, who orbited the moon while the first landing took place, said "Far from feeling lonely or abandoned, I feel very much part of what is taking place on the lunar surface… The venture has been structured for three men, and I consider my third to be as necessary as either of the other two…" The 'astronaut skills' tests are based around Tim Peake, the British man who has been selected to go to the International Space Station in 2015 for a 6 month mission. The information tells the girls that he survived 8 months of interviews and psychological tests and medical examinations to get through a field of 8,000 applicants.

"Imagine." says Rita,impressed.

"Yeah. Makes getting into uni look easy!" Priya replies.

The girls find that the lockers are in the same area as the loos and baby changing facilities, called a 'baby pod'. They take the opportunity quickly to inspect the disabled toilet where, Ben has told them, the police think a struggle took place. As well as the usual facilities, it has mirrors on the wall with wavy edges, fitting the space age theme. There are no signs of any struggle now.

The grey lockers are stacked three high against a wall.Rita takes the key, noting the number and finding the relevant door. She puts the key in the lock and, just as she is turning it, a hand reaches down on to her shoulder, making her jump with surprise.

"Excuse me, young lady." says a tall security guard looming over her in his pale blue uniform. "I see you are opening that locker. I wonder it I could check with you what's in it and if you would accompany me to the staff room."

Rita and Priya are speechless. They had not expected this!

"Okay." says Rita, "Let's see what's in here and then we can discuss it."

She opens the grey door under the intense gaze of Priya and the security guard, not sure what she is expecting to see. At first she thinks the interior is empty. There seems to be nothing there. Then she realises there is something. A single piece of paper is lying flat on the base of the locker. She goes to touch it but the security man says "I think I'll do that" and he reaches in with gloved hands to remove the paper.

"Just in case there are any useful fingerprints" he says. "Now let's take this upstairs to the staff office and call the police shall we? They warned me to expect someone to turn up with the key." and the security guard tries to turn them towards the stairs in a way which indicates there is no room for argument.

Rita and Priya, however, stop and look questioningly at each other. Should they trust this man?

"I think I'd prefer to talk to Sergeant Griffiths. I'll call him from here." Rita says and scrolls through her phone to find the number.

The security man, a curly haired individual in his early forties, sighs and folds his arms after making a 'go ahead if you must' gesture with his right hand. Meanwhile he has placed the sheet of paper taken from the locker into a clear plastic folder. Rita explains to the Sergeant, when she gets through to him, where she and Priya are and that a security guard is with them. Then the three of them move to a quiet area and she puts the Sergeant on loudspeaker.

"Well Rita." says the Sergeant. "What are you up to now?" (His deprecating tone reminds Rita of his reaction when she told him about Mrs Cummings. "We have a serious murder inquiry to investigate. I can't be worrying about little old ladies who go missing!" he had said, telling her that another officer was dealing with the disappearance.

"You've been keeping an eye on the locker?" Rita asks accusingly.

"Of course we have. It was the only one with the key missing. So we thought it might be relevant. We opened it and copied the original sheet of paper but we thought we'd see who came looking… and it turned out to be you!" the police officer tells her.

"How did you get the key by the way?" asks the security guard.

"Mr Gregson gave it to me." says Rita addressing her phone and Sergeant Griffiths rather than the security guard whose name, according to the badge on his uniform, is Ian. "You know, the man who told me about the missing old lady?" she refrains from reminding the Sergeant how dismissive he had been when told of Maureen Cummings' disappearance and the link with the Space Centre.

"Well?" Sergeant Griffiths is defensive. "Do you know what it means, the message on the paper?"

"Gives us a chance!" says Rita as she and Priya peer down at the script.

"It seems to be a list of numbers." she tells Sergeant Griffiths. "With a few letters added."

"Maybe it's some sort of code?" puts in Priya "A combination for a safe?"

"Maybe." replies the police officer from the phone, "But where is the safe in that case? There isn't one at the Centre or the Home."

The girls shrug.

"Okay if we take a copy?" says Rita "We might think what it means later."

"Yes that's fine," says the Sergeant "and thanks for your help, girls." he sounds genuinely grateful this time "You can let them go now Ian." he ends the conversation.

So Ian allows Rita to take a picture of the short message on her iPad. Then she and Priya go to sit in the café area to see if they can crack the code.

***

The café is like a conservatory with glass windows and rows of red tables and chairs. In one corner is the bottom part of a rocket which thrusts its way upwards through the ceiling to higher floors in the rocket tower. From the rocket engines every ten minutes or so, after a count-down that draws children to the foot of the rocket in excitement, the engines 'fire' as if for take off and that area of the café fills with 'smoke' made from dry ice. Rita and Priya smile at the drama created and the enjoyment it gives to enthusiasts of all heights and ages.

The message on the paper reads –
H/16A/85S/92I/86N'

"Is it directions?" suggests Priya, pointing to the N and S in case they signify north and south.

"Pretty odd ones if so." says Rita.

"A computer password maybe? They always recommend a mixture of numbers, letters and symbols?" is Priya's next suggestion.

"Possibly," concedes Rita, "but what computer? Sorry to keep dissing your ideas, keep them coming." she says as she pulls her phone from her bag to use the calculator.

"If I add the numbers it comes to 279. If I multiply them it makes..." she pauses to punch more numbers into the calculator, ("Come on Rachel Riley!" Priya mutters, thinking Rita sounds like she is on Countdown)

Rita goes on, "10,760,320" her shoulders slump in disappointment. The note doesn't make sense and she had thought they would find something really useful.

"It's so wack!" she exclaims, borrowing a phrase from her younger brother. Then she has another idea," Maybe the numbers stand for letters. But if so we're stuck as we don't know which letters each number represents. We need a code breaking machine like Alan Turing invented to crack the Germans' Enigma code!" Rita rattles on ('It must be terrifying to be inside your head!' Priya thinks.)

"Can we make an anagram with just the letters?" is Priya's next suggestion as the Thurable rocket fires up again to the sound of excited squeals.

After a few minutes the girls have come up with words like 'his', 'shin', 'is', 'ias', 'in', 'an' and 'has'.

"Mmmn. None of those looks hopeful." Rita and Priya agree.

"None of it makes sense." Rita says, cast down again.

"Maybe she was just losing it," Priya suggests.

"I just think she wasn't?" Rita disagrees. "I think she knew enough about what was going on to leave a proper clue. Why else go to the trouble of leaving a key for Mr Gregson?" she closes her iPad.

"Come on, let's think about it some more in the car. We have to find the answer!"

Chapter

8

"Houston, Tranquility Base here. The Eagle has landed."

Neil Armstrong, 20th June 1969
on landing on the moon.

Monday, July 14th 2014 2.30pm

"You two again?" says Michael Simmonds the next day, speaking weakly from his hospital bed where a bag of blood hangs on a stand to his left, slowly dripping into his system. "Can't a man get any peace? This is a hospital after all!"

Priya and Rita had checked in on the Maternity ward. The baby has developed an infection so, in Priya's words, Meera's bedside is 'anxiety central' and extra visitors are not welcome either there or in the neonatal unit. Everyone is hoping the baby is the fighter that Jai has been boasting about. Priya's mother is so worried she has taken herself off to the temple. So the girls had asked at the desk about Michael Simmonds and were directed to the Mens' Surgical ward.

"May as well try and talk to him." Rita had said when Priya queried whether this was a good idea.

The girls look at each other, then back to the bed that lies between them.

"We don't want to distress you." Priya says.

"We're just trying to help." Rita adds.

"Okay, okay" Michael utters, "I give in!" he shakes his head, "Find a chair and tell me what you want, but only after you refill my water jug." he extracts a price.

Priya takes the empty jug and goes in search of a water supply. Rita gathers two chairs from the pile in the corner of the six bay hospital ward. Each bay has pale blue curtains which can be drawn round the bed. At present the bay in the corner is shrouded over and quiet medical voices can be heard speaking as if they are conducting some tests on the patient. The other bays are open and four men, apart from Michael, of varying ages, sit up sprightly or slump like dolls depending on how they are feeling. The other patients have visitors, an older Asian man has several women fussing by his bedside and talking among themselves, not addressing the patient at all, a situation he seems content with, while a young white man has a female visitor with a toddler who plays on the floor with a set of toy cars which he sometimes sends whizzing across the ward floor. An older lady sits quietly by the man asleep opposite Michael and a middle aged man chats to a similar looking chap in the bed next to him.

Priya returns with the jug and pours Michael Simmonds a glass of water.

"I'm Rita Patel." says Rita when they sit down, "And this is my friend Priya Shah."

"Why are you here? In this hospital? Are you following me?" Michael says distrustfully, his Birmingham accent sounding strange in a Leicester hospital bed.

"Oh no!" Rita's tone is reassuring. "We were here to visit Priya's sister, she's just had a baby, it was a coincidence that we saw you when you were admitted."

Michael looks puzzled and disbelieving at this. "Uhuh." he says sceptically.

Rita embarks on an explanation. "Priya recently attended a post-mortem – she wants to study medicine -"

"Yes I know," Michael interrupts impatiently, "You saw a body and then you saw me and thought we might be related. The police explained that much…"

"The police have been here?" asks Rita.

"Oh yes," says Michael Simmonds sardonically, "It's not

enough that I get stabbed in the street for no apparent reason and end up in Leicester Infirmary, not only do the police have no idea who did it but they come badgering me for my DNA over some bloke…" his accent is stronger as he delivers this tirade, then he sinks back against the pillows.

"So how are you?" Priya thinks it may help to show an interest. "Can we get you anything? Is anyone coming to see you?" Priya realises she has asked too many questions at once. Michael Simmonds blinks and breathes out slowly while a tall black female nurse, with curly hair in a knot at the base of her neck, and black framed spectacles on her nose, comes to check on his blood transfusion bag. "Another twenty minutes" the nurse says and moves on in a business-like way to another bed.

"You're obviously not going to leave me alone 'til I tell you what I know." he says, turning towards Priya.

"I'd like some digestive biscuits from the shop if you can, the food here isn't very sustaining. If my parents can get here tomorrow they may bring me something. They don't drive so they'll have to come by train."

Michael grimaces a little as he tries to sit up. Priya stands to help him, adjusts the angle of the bed with the automatic control, and rearranges his pillows. As he moves, the girls can see across his back, under his gown, a bandaged area that passes round his middle and they exchange concerned looks.

"What do the doctors say?" Priya asks him when he is settled.

"Bloody lucky!" Michael Simmonds exclaims. "Deep wound they had to clean and stitch under general anaesthetic once they'd stopped the bleeding – that's why I'm having a top-up." he points to the red bag which is starting to sag now it is emptying.

"No major organs hit. They're keeping me in just in case the kidneys have been affected, but I reckon I'll (he says this as 'Oill') be fine."

"So how come you are in Leicester? And what happened?" Rita asks, while Priya makes a point of looking at the time, worried about tiring the injured man.

"I do busking, as you know," he looks piercingly at both girls, "In Birmingham. That's where I live. I have a flat above a music shop. I give music lessons. I teach pupils to play the trumpet." he stops, apparently finding the effort of talking is greater than he expected. Michael Simmonds takes another sip of water.

"I decided to come over here for a change. I haven't been to Leicester in ages, and I won't be coming back!" he says vehemently. "I set up in Town Hall Square, by the big lion fountain, you know." Priya and Rita nod. The brown fountain with its spouting lions sits in the middle of the square which has the Victorian Town Hall at one end. As well as a centre for the Council this is also the City's Registry Office and on many days civil partnership and wedding parties of all kinds can be seen trooping in and out and posing for photographs against the background of the fountain and the flower beds of the square. Once Priya had seen an Asian wedding go into the building as a white wedding came out. The demur bride in her red sari and the ladies in her party in their highly decorated saris of many colours had contrasted with the skimpy white dress of the bride in the other party, whose arms and cleavage were on show as were those of several of her female wedding guests. She wakes from her memories of this scene to hear Michael Simmonds say.

"So I hadn't been there long, about 10 minutes, when a voice – I couldn't place exactly where in the Square he was – said "Oi, Steve, I want a word with you!" then before I could move, two men came up to me. One said "You don't double cross Jake", at least I think that's what he said, and the other hit me and knocked me down. Then just as I was passing out I felt the first one hit me in the stomach. At least I thought he hit me but he must have had a knife and stabbed me.

Next thing I'm in an ambulance. Turns out a passing doctor probably saved my life, she put something on me to stem the bleeding." He stops talking, shaking at the memory.

"What do the police think?" Rita questions.

"Random attack. Nutters. Racists. They don't have a clue." he says dismissively.

"The attackers were white?" Rita checks.

"I think so, yeah, I don't remember much. Dark clothes, maybe a hat?"

"A cap you mean?" Rita asks.

"No, more wide brimmed, and a long black coat."

Priya thinks, that's unusual, especially in this very warm weather, why would anyone wear a coat?

"We'll get your biscuits." Priya says signalling to Rita that they've tired Michael enough. "Okay." says Rita, "And we'll come and see you tomorrow!" she promises.

"If you must!" says Michael grudgingly, although he has been glad of the company for a few moments.

"Just one thing." Rita adds, ignoring Priya's warning look, "Why do you think they called you Steve?"

"Oh, I have an idea about that." says Michael Simmonds mysteriously but his eyes are drooping and he clearly needs to sleep.

Chapter

9

*"The probability of success is difficult to estimate; but if
we never search the chance of success is zero."*
Quote from a paper of September 1959
'Searching for Interstellar Communications'
by Giuseppe Cocconi and Philip Morison.

Tuesday, July 15th 2014 2.30pm

The next day, Priya and Rita make a quick call at Meera's
bedside again where the news about the baby is better ("But
still no visitors, just lucky me!" says Meera looking very
tired, "He needs my milk but I have to express it, honestly
I get no rest!"). Jai is at work ("I'll need the time off when
the baby comes home") and he is adding to the tension by
phoning Meera and waking her up. Mrs Shah is still fussing
about a name ("You should call him something, it doesn't
seem right.")

Meanwhile, as they sit in the waiting area for the mens
ward to be ready for visitors – there seems to be a bit of a
delay - Priya is scrolling through her phone. Rita notices this
– is she Snapchatting Ben? - and tries to get Priya's attention.

"I've done some research into the Jewish population in
Leicester like I said I would." Rita says. "I thought I might
use it as a topic for study at University, the history of Jews
settling in the UK, why they came to certain areas, why they
left."

"Great!" says Priya who is interested on Ben's behalf. As
she has told Rita, Ben has said that he has few Jewish friends
and that his father wonders if there will be many Jews left in
Leicester soon.

"So there have never been many Jews in Leicester, and the number is going down." Rita confirms.

"Why is the museum in town called the Jewry Wall museum then?" Priya wants to know. "Surely that means something?"

"No one knows exactly, but a Jewish connection isn't the likeliest explanation." Rita disappoints her, "As you know, the museum houses archaeological collections relating to the City up to the Middle Ages, and includes a really good example of a mosaic and some Roman wall paintings."

Priya nods to encourage Rita, although she has not really noticed what is kept in the museum.

"The wall is Roman, of course, it was part of the Roman baths and the wall is one of the largest pieces of Roman building surviving in the country. Did you know it is over 9 meters high?"

Priya looks impressed to please her friend and takes her comb from her bag to stroke it through her pony tail while Rita speaks.

"A lot of the stone from the Roman wall was re-used to build churches like St Nicholas church which was built by the Anglo Saxons in the middle of town. The bit that's left of the wall may have been named after the medieval Jewish community, but this does not seem very likely."

"So why then?" Priya is puzzled.

"I think this is the best theory." Rita tells her, "It was referred to as the 'Jury Wall' by William Stukeley in his map of 1722, which might refer to the 24 Borough councillors who used to meet in the church yard in medieval times; they were called 'Jurats'. I think the jurat theory is a good one as there seems to be no link between the wall and any Jewish quarter."

"Oh." Priya is disappointed. "So how many Jewish people settled here? What was the highest number?" she asks.

"The records are vague." Rita tells Priya, "The earliest

evidence for Jews in Leicester dates from 1185. The evidence relates to pledges and money lending. The Jews here seem to have had links with Jews in Lincoln and Nottinghamshire. There was a small Jewish community in the City by the end of the twelfth century. A guy called Ranulf, the Earl of Chester, got royal authority for them to be unmolested. Ranulf held the authority in custody for Simon de Montfort."

"The one who they say called the first Parliament?" Priya remembers Rita has told her about him, and that his statue in one of the four stone figures on the Haymarket Memorial Clock Tower in the city centre.

"Well he wasn't nice to the Jews." Rita tells Priya, "In August 1231 he got his estates back - remember he was sometimes friends with the King, Henry III, and sometimes arguing and fighting with him? He issued a charter banishing Jews from living in the liberty of the town. Although some found refuge in another part of Leicester, by the end of 1231 their expulsion was effective and they ceased to exist in the town for hundreds of years."

"Golly." says Priya, still tending to her hair; she had not realised things had been so bad.

"The first evidence for the modern Jewish community here dates from the middle of the 1800s. There are records of a partnership between an Israel Hart of Canterbury and a Joseph Levy of Leicester. Hart moved to Leicester and the Leicester Hebrew Congregation starts to be mentioned in the Jewish Chronicle around then. At the end of the 19th century 10 families were sent to Leicester, probably at the instigation of Hart and Levy, and a new synagogue was built and opened in 1895. The population grew during the Second World War, peaking at about 1,500 in 1945, but it was down to a few hundred by 2004. Newspaper reports recently say the population is shrinking fast, and unlikely to survive in the City in the face of increasing anti-semitic attacks."

"No way! Really?" Priya is outraged.

"'Fraid so. There was an attack on a Rabbi, and nowadays most Leicester Jews choose not to dress outwardly to show their faith in case they are set upon. The Synagogue was sold in 2011. History is repeating itself and the Jews are effectively being expelled again."

Rita's flow is curtailed as they realise that visiting time on the Mens' Surgical ward is beginning at last and the gaggle of visitors who had been aimlessly staring at the posters on the notice board or idly watching the lift go up and down moves as one mass into the body of the ward where the men Rita and Priya had seen the previous day are all still in their beds, apart from the elderly gentleman who is sitting on a chair wearing a rather smart red dressing gown.

"Hi, you two, thanks for the biccies." is Michael's greeting (they had left some packets in his bedside cabinet while he slept.) He gestures to them to pull up chairs.

"Feeling any better?" asks Priya.

"It helps to sleep," he admits, "but it's hard to do that in here, they are always waking you for one reason or another."

"Are they still worried about your kidneys?" Priya wants to know.

"They are going to do more tests tomorrow, to make sure everything's okay." he tells her.

"Food any better?" Rita queries, noticing a plate with a plastic cover sitting on Michael's table, awaiting collection.

The patient screws up his nose, "If you like eating breadcrumbs – everything's covered in them - and the so-called roast potatoes are very hard. I don't know how the chaps with poor teeth manage." he smiles and when he does so it lifts his whole face, making it seem kinder and softer;it is hard to tell if the harsher countenance he wears most of the time is part of his character or to do with the pain and discomfort he is in, Priya thinks.

"What about your parents? Heard from them?" Priya asks him.

"They may come later on. A neighbour might bring them." Michael sighs.

"You were going to tell us why the people who attacked you called you Steve." Rita can wait no longer.

"Oh yeah," Michael wriggles to get more comfortable under the sheets. "I had a brother, have I suppose, did have if he's the guy in the paper."

"How come? What do you mean?" Priya wants to know.

"We were, are, twins, but our real mother, who was in her teens when she has us, couldn't cope, at least that what my Mum and Dad tell me. So we were put into care. I remember Steve and I being together in a couple of foster homes, and at the childrens home, before Mum and Dad said they would have me. I was fostered by them at first, then they adopted." As he recalls his childhood, Michael's Birmingham accent becomes more obvious. His unfocussed eyes stare across the ward as if recreating scenes in his mind.

"So you were both in care." Rita says slowly, absorbing the information.

"Where did you live, before you were adopted?" Priya wants to know.

"Oh, I've always lived in Birmingham. We were born in Handsworth." Michael says, mentioning an area close to the city centre. "I don't remember anything before I was about two and a half, when I fell off a swing and broke my arm, that's my first memory. We were with a nice couple then, Aunty Mary and Uncle Joe, but it must only have been temporary. We stopped with various families – lots of brothers and sisters to get to know - but it never lasted long; the rejection was hard to take. I guess boy twins are a handful. Soon we were back in the childrens home again."

"What was that like?" Rita wants to know.

"When you're three or four you don't really question do you?" is how Michael responds, "You just accept, you probably think everyone has the same experience, if you think about it all, except that I did know, some part of me knew, that other children went home to mummies and daddies, say after the Christmas party or on their birthdays, while we went to the Home. Don't get me wrong, they weren't cruel or anything, at least not to us, but it wasn't the same as having your own mum and dad. I knew that when my parents … I realised the difference." His voice trails off with the memory.

Then Michael coughs, wincing slightly at the effort, and continues, 'The childrens' home was in a big house - it seemed big to us at any road - with blue lino on the floors and red tiles on the walls – that deep red that's almost brown, and the tiles had patterns indented on them – still makes me shudder to think about those tiles, I'd never decorate with the colour. There was a lot of lining up as I recall; line up to eat, line up to clean your teeth, line up to go to bed. You were always in a queue. Boys stood one side, girls the other. Me and Steven – Steve - kept together when we could, and we slept in the same room, with two other boys I think, I don't remember their names. I remember the birthday parties – there was always someone having one and we got jelly and ice cream - and the punishments! If you made the carers cross they'd lock you in the cupboard. Steve got locked in there a few times, I used to sit outside and talk to him, until I got shooed away."

"Were you identical twins?" Rita asks breaking into his reverie.

"I s'pose. Never really thought about it. Yes we must have been." Michael starts to sound more certain, "People would muddle us up. The carers made us wear different socks, mine were blue, his were brown." He looks surprised as if he has only just recalled this detail.

"Did Steve get into trouble a lot then?" Priya wants to know more.

"He was always more reckless than I was. He'd push it with the carers, he'd take food he wasn't meant to, keep toys which should have gone back in the toy box after playtime, that sort of thing, nothing bad, just disobedient ,and in a Home you need order, I can see that now, otherwise you'd soon have chaos. Pass me a biscuit would you please? They're in the cabinet." he adds to Priya who jumps up to oblige.

"Is that why your Mum and Dad chose you, not Steve?" Rita presses.

A pained look crosses Michael's face, "Maybe... We don't talk about it… I missed him terribly. Although I liked being with my Mum and Dad it was like I'd lost part of myself. Know what I mean?" the girls nod, trying to understand.

"My parents already had three children – girls – and they only had room for one more. They did explain that to me, a bit later. It made me sad to think of Steve on his own in the Home. But Mum and Dad said maybe another couple would come and take him to their house, so then I thought of him like me, with a nice family, having his own toys to play with and no one telling him off for keeping them."

"But you don't know what became of him?" Rita checks.

"Not a clue. I'd forgotten to be honest – well not exactly forgotten just pushed it to the back of my mind – until you two showed up with the newspaper clipping…" Michael tells them between bites of biscuit.

"Do you know what your original surname was? I assume it was changed on adoption?" Rita has her iPad out to make notes. "Yeah, Bailey. I was Michael Bailey and he was Steven Bailey." Michael slumps back on the pillow, tiredness starting to affect him.

"Did you tell the police about Steve?" Rita wants to know.

"I don't know. I don't think so. It was all a bit confused. I only put the bits together while I've been lying here. Do you think I should say anything? I don't want to get Steve into trouble, unless he's the one you saw…" he turns to Priya who nods,

"I am afraid it probably was him. The DNA will confirm

if there is a connection between you. It looks to me like Steve may have got you into trouble rather than the other way round." Priya tells him, as Michael hands round the shortbread again.

✳✳✳

"So what will the DNA show?" Rita asks in the lift as she and Priya leave the building. "Is the DNA of twins identical, if they are identical twins?"

"For most purposes the genomes are the same." explains Priya, "Non identical twins share between 50% and 75% of the same genetic code and identical twins share 99.99%."

"So if twins are identicial, there's no way of distinguishing between them. If they did a crime, for example, and there was DNA evidence, you couldn't tell which of them did it?" Rita is interested.

Priya nods her head. Trust Rita to want to know that! "Well they have unique fingerprints, of course, so that can help the police. But where there is no fingerprint evidence then in the past the police have been stumped; they may know one twin did the crime but they can't prove which. Recently, though, scientists have found, if they look very carefully, that there are some little differences in the DNA sequences. It's like a nature/nurture thing. Even though identical twins have essentially the same genetic material they bump around in the womb and each is in a slightly different position so maybe that affects certain things?" Priya tries to explain, "No one really knows for sure how it happens, but the point is that there <u>are</u> differences in the codes if you look closely enough. Which costs more money of course, so the police don't do it often. But it means that some of those unsolved cases from the past could now be solved."

"So if the body is that of Michael's identical twin, his DNA will clinch it? It will give the police an identity to go on?" Rita

81

is getting excited now.

"That's right. One mystery solved and another created." Priya replies enigmatically.

"You're right." says Rita, "What life did Steve lead? Why was he at the Space Centre and why was he killed?"

Tuesday, 15th July 2014 7.30pm

Mr and Mrs Simmonds are with their son when Rita and Priya return for a quick visit that evening. "Mum and Dad, these are my friends, Rita and Priya." Michael makes the introductions from his hospital bed.

Both parents are smartly dressed. Michael's mother wears extensive make up high on her cheek bones and over her eyelids and has silver jewellery over a purple top and a purple skirt with a flowery pattern on it; she has a leather jacket balanced on her shoulders. Her black hair is braided. Mr Simmonds' black hair is greying on top; he wears brown trousers and a white shirt and carries a tweed jacket, the hospital is too warm to wear it.

Michael says cheerfully, "I'm hoping I can be discharged tomorrow!"

"Yes", Mrs Simmonds speaks, "We're staying in a hotel tonight so we can take him home. I don't want him travelling by himself, especially after what happened."

"I'll (Oi'll) be fine, honestly." Michael protests.

"Can't be too careful, son." says Mr Simmonds "I'll be glad to have you out of Leicester." ('As if it was a wild frontier town on the edge of anarchy', Rita thinks).

"We've been talking about Michael's family." Mr Simmonds says "Your sisters will be glad you're okay. As for that other fellow, whether or not it was your natural brother… is that the expression? We are sorry to hear what happened to him."

"We felt bad not being able to adopt both boys." Mrs Simmonds says, turning to Rita, and wringing her hands;

Rita can see silver rings on several of her fingers.

"Do you remember the name of Michael's mother?" Rita asks while Priya frowns, she is not sure this is the time to raise this question, but Rita thinks there may not be another occasion if Michael is being discharged. "Only it might help to establish the connection between Michael and the dead man, if there is any." she explains.

"I thought this might come up." Mrs Simmonds says reluctantly. She takes a piece of paper out of her green handbag and puts on reading glasses to peer at it.

"I suppose we always knew this day would come." says Mr Simmonds, "Only we didn't expect it to be beside Michael's hospital bed."

"Here." Michael's mother hands the piece of paper to him and says softly, "Helen, her name was Helen Bailey, I hope that helps you".

Tuesday, 15th July 2014 10pm

Later, alone at home Rita opens her iPad and notices that the code left by Mrs Cummings is still lurking there, unsolved. Rita tries the name "Helen Bailey" on Facebook. There are a few possibilities, but only one stands out. Rita is looking at a woman of the right age who has smiling pictures of herself standing with a choir at various venues. It does seem likely that she would be musical, she thinks, as Michael is so clearly talented in that direction. Should she mention this to Michael or not? Rita thinks she will check with Priya. Is it something mother and son would want, let alone his adoptive parents?

Chapter

10

"I see the moon like a clipped piece of silver. Like gilded bees the stars cluster round her."

Oscar Wilde

Thursday, 3rd July 2014 4pm

It is early July, and for A-level students like her the summer holidays have started early. Morwenna Maitland carefully closes the door of the basement flat where she lives with her parents, lifts her brown bag over her left shoulder to place it across her body and climbs the steps up to the ground floor. She moves deliberately, slower than her usual pace, a sign she has made a decision and is determined to carry it through. Pausing at the end of the drive, in the middle of which sits the sundial after which the bed and breakfast business is named, she stands in her purple leggings and acid yellow top to look back briefly. Morwenna tosses her head quickly so that her long fair hair swishes forwards and backwards. She strokes her hands over the top of her head and wriggles her body slightly as the tresses adjust themselves. The general effect is momentarily like that of a mermaid preening herself on a seabound rock. Satisfied, she moves on, scrolling through her contacts in her phone until she finds the number she wants.

"Jed. Come and get me?" her voice is childlike and whining, she wants Jed to know she's in trouble and needs help.

"I'll be outside Nico's." (this is the wine shop on the corner, near the Sundial Bed and Breakfast, which her mother runs) she tells the disembodied male voice which sounds surprised.

Morwenna can hear voices shouting in the background, so maybe he is with his mates, she thinks. But his response is what she wants to hear.

"Okay babe, give me 10."

Morwenna walks to the corner and uses the cash machine outside Nico's while she waits. Counting £100 into her purse, her mind is elsewhere, going through its own litany.

"I've had it with my parents. They just don't get me. Mum's too controlling. 'Where are you going? When will you be back? Shall I cook a meal?' She needs to get a life. Dad's never there, always working, or abroad, or doing jobs around Sundial to placate mum. No one listens to me. They don't get that I'm a grown up."

The notes safely stowed in her designer purse, she places it back inside the bag slung across her body, takes a deep breath and sighs. She stares out at the road, which is fairly quiet at this time of day, but she does not see the cars or notice the appreciative looks she is getting from a group of boys who walk by on their way to stock up on the chocolate and crisps which Nico sells alongside his supply of alcohol.

A motorbike draws up to the kerb beside her – a Harley Davidson with an England flag at the back - and the rider leans over to hand Morwenna a helmet which she places over her long hair with ease, having ridden Jed's bike several times before. "Hi." she says as she straddles the machine. Jed guns the throttle and they swoop away, like a swallow taking flight. After a few minutes of gliding along they are weaving their way through a queue of vehicles at a set of traffic lights when Morwenna leans forward to speak into Jed's ear.

"Where are we going?"

"Didn't I tell you?" Jed turns slightly to shout back over the roar of the bike, his Scottish accent quite pronounced,

"I'm kipping at Harry's now, Calvin kicked me out."

"Oh." Morwenna is a little taken aback, but as Jed has turned back to look at the road he does not see the surprised look on her face. This is not the romantic start to the next phase of her life which she had pictured.

"Harry's okay." Jed reassures her, "He'll be cool with you staying a coupla nights." And he revs up the engine again as they accelerate towards Blaby where Harry and his other half (Sandy) have a one bedroomed terraced house which fronts onto the main road.

"An adventure." Morwenna tells herself, "And one my parents will know nothing about!"

***

Having left the bike by the kerb, Jed and Morwenna take off their helmets and indulge in a slow long kiss on the pavement before breathlessly ringing the bell to be admitted to the house in Blaby by a less than friendly Sandy who has her arms folded.

"You'd best come in." is the most welcome she can muster as she mentally compares Morwenna's clear fresh complexion and rippling fair locks with her own more mottled skin and short stubbled hair which today is a red tone thanks to the addition of henna, but in recent weeks has been various shades from gothic black to brick brown. In her boots Morwenna is also a few inches taller than Sandy. She smiles shyly at the older woman, a look which usually works when she wants something, and the couple go past Sandy into the living room which Morwenna soon learns doubles as Jed's temporary bedroom.

"I'm on shift tonight. You coming with me?" Jed tells Morwenna, then to Sandy he says "I'll get us pizza first?"

"Okay." Sandy agrees. "Harry will be back in half an hour."

"Tandoori chicken for him, tuna and prawn for you and we'll have a vegetable feast." Jed recites the order.

"Can you call them up babe, there's the number" and he hands Morwenna a card from his pocket which has the details of 'Happypizzaco' printed on its yellow surface. When the call placed by Morwenna gets to the request for the delivery address, Jed recites it to Morwenna, standing close and twining his fingers between hers so that she struggles not to giggle.

"I've made tea." Sandy reappears bearing three chipped mugs on a tin tray. One advertises PG Tips, one is plain red and the third is from Llandudno. There is a packet of sugar and a spoon beside the mugs. The tea in each mug has been stirred and the scummy surface swirls like dirty bath water going down the plug hole. Morwenna sits on the plastic (leather effect) sofa next to Sandy, Jed squats on the spotted bean bag on the floor.

"I'm working nights." Sandy offers between sips, "So don't make a lot of noise in the morning. I'll be sleeping."

"Still at the supermarket?" Jed asks, knowing Sandy has been stacking shelves at Tesco for a couple of years now.

"Yeah. Pays the bills." Sandy says pointedly.

"Don't you mind working through the night?" Morwenna asks, wondering what that would be like.

"You get used to it." Sandy replies, "I like the peace and quiet." she makes another barbed remark as they hear Harry unlocking the front door.

"Hi Jed! Hi Morwenna!"

Harry's welcome is more fulsome than his partner's. He opens his arms to offer a hug which both stand to accept even though Morwenna has concerns about whether any oil or other dirt will transfer from his once orange (now mostly black) mechanic's overalls.

"I'll just get changed and make a cuppa." Harry says.

"Pizza coming!" Jed tells his back as he heads for the kitchen followed by Sandy. Even though they close the door and whisper, some of the couple's conversation, conducted as the kettle boils for Harry's tea, can be heard.

"How long are they staying?" Sandy, accusingly.

"He didn't really say." Harry, pathetically.

"You've got to put your foot down." Sandy, emphatically.

"I will." Harry, hesitantly.

"No, I mean it!" Sandy, vehemently.

"Okay, Okay." Harry being placatory.

"Jed's one thing, but two of them!" Sandy, indignantly "And it's not as if he makes a contribution."

"He is getting pizza isn't he?" Harry, pleadingly.

As if on cue, the door bell rings.

"Get that, babe," says Jed, and Morwenna goes to the door to take delivery of the pizzas and hand over one of the notes she recently obtained from the cash point.

She feels very adult striding back into the room bearing the food, and hands out the boxes like a waitress in a restaurant as Sandy and Harry enter the living room and settle on the sofa and a dining chair respectively. Sandy has brought in with her a roll of kitchen towel from which they tear pieces to wipe their greasy fingers and chins. Morwenna likes sharing her pizza with Jed, it makes her feel close to him and she gets a feeling of belonging from sitting with the other three as they munch on the cheese-laden slices.

Friday, 4th July 2014 3.30am

In the early hours of the next day, Morwenna and Jed return from the bar where he works in the centre of Leicester. It is 3.30am. They creep in quietly in order not to disturb Harry, although he will no doubt have heard the motorbike engine which heralded their return. They switch on the floor lamp in the corner – acquired by Sandy from a charity shop - and Morwenna clears away the pizza boxes while Jed unfolds the sofa and throws a pillow and a quilt onto it. Morwenna uses the downstairs bathroom and Jed rummages in his kit bag for a t-shirt she can wear overnight.

"Going for a slash." Jed says tiredly, rubbing his eyes with his hands, and by the time he returns to the room Morwenna is under the duvet, having draped her designer top over the back of a dining chair and the rest of her clothes on the seat.

"Budge up." Jed says. "Good to have you babe." he breathes into her hair as she leans her back against him and nestles her bum against his crotch. He stretches across her to put his palms on her breasts. Gradually his breathing deepens and his grip relaxes. Jed is asleep.

Friday, 4th July 2014 8.30am

Morwenna wakes to the roar of a refuse van outside, the yells of the operatives and the thud of bins being loaded onto the van for emptying and then dropped unceremoniously in the interests of efficiency at points in the street not strictly resembling where they were collected from. Later in the day will begin the ritual of each household scouring the road to find their own bin.

It is hard to tell what time it is and she curses that she took off her watch and left her phone in her bag. She must have been too tired to think properly when they got in. She had spent the evening in a corner of the bar while Jed served customers, occasionally sitting up at the bar when it was less busy, and sipping vodka and tonic.

The light from outside is filtered through orange curtains which only fit the bay window in places, leaving gaps at the curtain rail level. Jed is lying on Morwenna's right arm so that she cannot really feel it, but she is reluctant to move him, he seems so peaceful. In sleep his features relax and with his long black hair splayed on the pillow he looks younger than when he is tense behind the bar, trying to keep the customers happy, a job which gets harder as the evening goes by and the customers' consumption of alcohol is more evident in their behaviour and manner,

Still, the tips had been good last night. Some Americans

visiting Richard III sites had been generous and Jed had chatted to them about the bike rides he had taken in his twenties through South Dakota to San Francisco and on Route 66 through Oklahoma to Los Angeles. Morwenna had heard Sandy return, that must have been about 6.30am. Sandy was dropped off at the end of the road by a minibus run by the supermarket. Now Morwenna can hear someone in the kitchen next door making toast, presumably Harry on his way out to the garage down the road where he works. So maybe it was about 9 in the morning, she gueses? Morwenna gradually extracts her arm from under Jed, turns onto her side and is soon asleep again.

Friday, 4th July 2014 12.10pm

Morwenna wakes once more just after midday, uses the bathroom, and reverses the clothing process while Jed slumbers on. Then she makes them tea and uses up the last of the bread for toast which she and Jed consume on the sofa/bed. A lengthy and energetic bout of sex follows before they fold up the sofa. Sandy emerges at some point when they are distracted by their lovemaking and now goes out, making a point of slamming the front door shut after shouting "I'm going out to get bread!" Then they hear the rumble of a wheelie bin being put back in place followed by her footsteps receding towards the corner shop. Jed and Morwenna sink giggling and hugging onto the sofa.

"Gotta move on tomorrow babe." Jed breaks the news suddenly becoming serious as Morwenna strokes and bestows kisses on his tattoed forearms.

"Oh?" she stretches full length with her head on Jed's lap, looking up into his face. He bends to kiss her, his long hair tickling her face, his beard rubbing against her chin.

"Harry said one more night. Sandy is nay so keen on you staying." he explains not very gallantly.

"Where'll we go?" Morwenna opens her eyes wide, adding to the helplessness she is communicating by her supine posture.

"Camping." Jed is decisive, sitting up and pushing Morwenna off his lap.

"How? Where?" Morwenna straightens up and does the flicking trick with her hair to rearrange it.

"I've a tent." Jed announces, "And we can do the festivals. It'll be fun."

"Yeah." Morwenna is enthusiastic. This sounds more like the adventure she has been looking for. "I'll have to buy some more boots." she adds.

Saturday, 12th July 2014 7am

Morwenna wakes in a field. She smells wet grass, damp with early morning dew, and soil. There is a faint whiff of animal dung, probably from the cows in the next field, and a pigeon's insistent cry of "whoo whoo" can be heard. Her arms are pinned to their side in the narrowness of the sleeping bag she is sharing, the zip is on her left and Jed is on her right. He has his chin resting on her collarbone, the bristles of his beard gently digging into her skin as she breathes in and out. The sun glints through the gaps in the doorway of the tent but it is probably still quite early she thinks. The weather has been good so far, long hot days melting into light sultry evenings when it seems as if the sun hardly goes away. Funny how you do not notice it getting dark when you are outside all the time she thinks.

They had been told to leave the last camp site as they had not paid the entrance fee- Jed had found a hole in the fence and they had just walked through. They had joined in the music and the dancing. It was one of those new age festivals where you 'find yourself' through yoga or tantric sex or hypnotism. Morwenna had felt at home and cheerfully joined in various workshops and therapy sessions. She bought a pink kaftan and a scarf to help her blend in and was pleased with the 'Kate Moss' look she created wearing these with her new boots. Jed had not blended in so well, especially when he donned his black coat over his biker trousers and t-shirt, although his black hat, which he allowed Morwenna to wear when sitting on his shoulders to get a better view of the stage, made him look stylish. He had left Morwenna several times to meet up with his friends in the centre of Leicester. Eventually his coming and going had caught the interest of Security and the bouncers had moved them off the site. They had seen the best band anyway so no great loss they said to themselves.

Now they are in a field courtesy of a friendly and laid-back farmer who provides bread, cheese, eggs and milk from his farm shop at reasonable prices. Morwenna is getting good at preparing omelettes on the small primus stove they acquired at a hardware shop. She is learning what herbs to gather from the field edges, woods and pathways and she is also able to pick berries that look edible. The summer sun, after a winter of unprecedented rainfall, seems to be stimulating nature into plentiful production. Sellers by the roadside have strawberries on offer, for example, as well as runner beans and courgettes.

Closing her eyes to sleep a little longer, Morwenna remembers she must ask Jed to return her bank card. He took it with him on his last trip to meet his friends, so he could get some cash if he saw a chance; (she had told him the PIN). He had given her £20 on his return. It seemed a good arrangement.

Later, Morwenna wakes as the sleeping bag rocks and shakes with Jed's waking movements. He places one socked leg on the top of the bag, then the other, and drags his jeans from the top of his kit bag to pull them on, followed by a t-shirt.

"Going for a slash." he says, untying the tent door and disappearing into the bright light of the day.

Morwenna sits up and stretches before taking the kaftan and pulling it over her head and then stepping into her boots. She can hear Jed's voice in heated conversation. She looks in her bag and realises he must be using her phone. She had wondered the previous day what had happened to it. She had worried that she had lost it. She is confirmed in her belief when the phone in Jed's hand rings and it uses 'Wake Me Up!' By Avicii, which she had downloaded.

"I'll be there in a hour." she can hear Jed saying, "I'll have to bring the bird." 'So they are going somewhere?' she thinks. Ten minutes later, biting from chunks of bread as they work, they take the folded tent and all their possessions to the bike, and load them and themselves onto it. Morwenna, as she climbs on the Harley Davidson, remembers Jed still has her phone and bank card, but he is in a hurry to be off so she does not trouble him about it.

The bike gathers speed on the A46 and Jed opens it up some more on the dual carriageway. Morwenna notices they are leaving Nottinghamshire and aiming for Leicester again. At some traffic lights they pick up signs to Abbey Park and then Jed turns down Exploration Drive and they arrive at the car park of the National Space Centre. Morwenna vaguely recalls going there on a school trip once, but cannot remember much about it, except maybe that's where she got the stars which she stuck on the ceiling above her bed in her parents' flat (as she is beginning to think of it). They glowed in the dark and she liked to see them when she went to sleep. She smiles at the memory as Jed indicates she should get off the bike and wait for him. He strides over to the group of fellow bikers gathered in a corner of the car park.

Jed has not explained why they are here and Morwenna does not expect him to. He needs to meet his friends, then they can make their way to the next gig or festival she thinks.

The good weather looks like it will hold for a bit longer so they may as well make the most of it. Bits of the discussion Jed and his friends are having drift over to Morwenna.

"What's he told the fuzz?"

"Has he grassed?"

"Do you think it's in there?"

"What if the feds find it?"

"Twenty grand down the swannee."

"Jake's not going to be happy."

"See you in the Square on Monday."

"Reporters over there. Let's split."

Then Jed returns and motions that she needs to climb aboard quickly, hardly giving her time to put on her helmet. It occurs to Morwenna that while they are in the area they could call in on Sundial. She would like her parents to see how grown up she is, for them to see her as an adult in a proper relationship, but Jed is concentrating on the road and has a plan for them, she can tell, so she hangs on and says nothing, waiting to see where the next part of the adventure will be.

Thursday, 17*th* July 2014 3pm

Morwenna is strolling by the side of Leicester Market, browsing the clothes stalls which are collected there. She sees several tops she would like to buy, but she only has a few pounds in her pocket and she cannot afford them all. Jed still has her bank card and her phone. She finds it strange that she likes the tops when she is used to wearing designer labels and the store of choice has been where she worked, until she went away with Jed, Jack Wills. She decides on an orange patterned top and hands over most of the cash she has on her. Then she walks along the cobbled surface, taking in the noise and bustle, the colours of the fruit and vegetables, the sweet and sour smells, the cries and shouts of the sellers. She vaguely hopes that she may bump into her mother. Athena sometimes shops there for fresh vegetables for the soups she likes to make for her guests.

Morwenna crosses the road towards Town Hall Square where Jed is meeting his friends.It seems to be a popular meeting place for them as it is central and they come from all sides of the City. When she sees what is happening, she starts to speed up and the plastic carrier bag swings by her side and knocks against her leg. Morwenna realises she is arriving just in time. An ugly scene is starting to develop. Parked against the kerb are a number of motor bikes, Jed's among them. Propped against a bench is a push bike. Two boys are sitting on the bench with McDonalds drinks. The leather-clad bikers are standing in front of the boys and as the latter, feeling confronted, stand up to defend themselves, their drinks slide to the ground. Now the bikers are shouting angrily at the boys.

"You pair again!"

"What are you hiding?"

"You saw something?"

One of the youths tries to diffuse the situation but it only makes it worse. "Steady on granddad! What's your problem? We don't know anything."

"Don't get clever with me!"

One of the bikers seizes one of the boys by the throat, another takes a swing at the boy in a t-shirt with a penguin on it. The boy ducks and rugby tackles the biker around the knees, bringing him crashing down. A policeman who was standing on the opposite side of the road radios for help. Morwenna can see as she approaches that Jed still has hold of one of the boys by the throat and is squeezing harder.

"Stop! Stop!" Morwenna runs across the road, thinking she may recognise one of the boys.

"Stop!" she raises her hands in the air, dropping her new top in the process, and takes hold of Jed's tattooed arms.

"Let him go! Let him go!" she shouts.

"Fuzz!" shouts one of the bikers as the police officer crosses to the Square and a siren can be heard approaching.

"Scarper!" The bikers run to their machines, Morwenna is torn between helping the boy who was being half strangled and following Jed. She chooses Jed, scooping up the new top from the pavement as she runs behind him to the Harley Davidson, scrambles aboard, and the bikers leave the scene like a flock of geese hastily migrating.

Chapter

11

"The pursuit of the good and evil are now linked in astronomy as in almost all science. The fate of human civilisation will depend on whether the rockets of the future carry the astronomer's telescope or a hydrogen bomb."

Bernard Lovell, 1959

Thursday, July 17th 2014 5pm

"Tell me again what Athena said and why we need to go to Sundial?" Priya asks as she enters Rita's house in Elm Drive. Her mother has dropped her off on the way to see her new grandchild, still in hospital, all thoughts of her online business shelved, Priya notes.

"Athena was in a terrible state." says Rita referring to their friend at whose B & B the girls had worked the previous summer. Rita and Priya are in Rita's room now while she scoops everything she needs into her Cath Kidston bag - iPhone, iPad and keys to the Peugeot. Priya notices some paint charts scattered on the pink bed.

"You are really thinking of decorating?" she asks and her friend says "I might. I've had enough of this pink. You'd help me wouldn't you?"

"Sure." says Priya, thinking her own parents would not be keen if she suggested painting her room.

In the car they pull away from the kerb, heading to the Knighton area where Sundial is situated.

"How long has Morwenna been missing?" Priya wants to know, referring to Athena's daughter who is the same age as the girls and until recently went to the sixth form of a local private school. Morwenna, Priya recalls, has long blond hair and likes to wear fashionable clothes. She prefers working in fashion shops to helping in her parents' business.

Arriving at Sundial in the late afternoon, Priya watches in admiration as Rita neatly parks the car in one of the spaces by the sundial, which sits in the centre of what was once the front garden of the four storey Edwardian house and is now an open area for parking. Priya and Rita descend the steps to the basement flat where Morwenna lives with her parents. Athena, whose guests sleep and eat breakfast in the upper parts of the house, has seen them arrive and opens the flat door. Priya is alarmed to see her usual calm and orderly demeanour has been replaced by a disshelved and distracted look, as if Athena had been standing in a wind tunnel. Athena's face is pale – she is probably not sleeping thinks Rita - and her auburn hair hangs loose and untidy. She wears shorts and a t-shirt and has flip-flops on her feet. Normally Rita and Priya revere Athena and envy the artistic ease of her appearance, but not today.

"Come in! Come in!" Athena is welcoming and beckons them across the threshold to the flat which has a cosy, cabin-like feel to it with books lining most of the walls, a honey oak wooden floor covered with rugs, a large welcoming cream sofa to the left of them, a chest-shaped coffee table in the middle of the room and a brick fire place to their right, with several pictures arranged above it, all of sea scenes. Morwenna's father's law books occupy some of the shelves, he is an intellectual property lawyer with a local firm and often works abroad. Priya can also see sets of Austen, Trollope and Dickens as well as more modern authors but her examination is cut short by Athena who is offering them elderflower cordial which the girls gladly accept; it has been another warm day and they feel a little dehydrated.

"When did you last see Morwenna?" Rita asks when they are sitting down, the girls on the sofa, Athena in a leather armchair.

"Two weeks ago!" Athena wails. "I thought she just meant she was – you know – going out. She said – we had a row about her boyfriend, well he's not a boy he's 33 - Jed, 15 years older than her! – And then she just said "Well I'm going then!" and walked out of the flat. She didn't have anything with her, no coat, not that you'd need one with the lovely weather we've been having, but no bag either – well she had her handbag- the brown leather one she wears across her body?" Athena mimes the bag as if it will jog their memories; Priya and Rita nod. They recall the bag.

"And then she didn't come back for supper… and I looked in her room and her passport and her purse are missing… Oh dear!" Athena wrings her hands. "I don't know what to think! If anything happens to her!" Athena leaves the thought unsaid and her tea undrunk and, looking around the flat, Priya and Rita can see this is not the first time this has happened; there are several half full cups marooned on the floor and the table.

"What does Edward say?" Priya wants to know, inquiring about Athena's husband.

"Oh, the usual. 'Don't worry. She'll come back when she's ready'. It's all right for him, he's hundreds of miles away."

"When is he due back?" Rita asks, thinking that Athena could so with some moral support.

"Next week." Athena tells them. "He says he can't get back sooner as he has a deal to finish," she says, narrowing her lips in disapproval as she speaks.

"And her phone? Is she answering her phone?" is Rita's next question. "Not to me she isn't!" is Athena's anguished reply. "Oh I wish I knew she was okay."

"Well one of us can try." offers Priya wanting to offer some hope. "She might talk to us, what's her number?" and Athena picks up her phone, which lies on the coffee table as if awaiting a call from her daughter, and she forwards the number to Rita's phone.

"The police…" Athena begins to say.

"You've involved the police?" Rita's tone is surprised.

"They were no help!" Athena almost spits out. "They say she's an adult and she's only been gone a few days. What if she ends up in a ditch, or dead in the boot of a car?"

"Now that's not likely." Priya tries to calm the older woman. "You think she's with this man Jed?"

"Yes, well that was my next thought. She has spent the night with him a few times – I know, I know!" Athena interprets the surprised looks on the girls' faces as disapproving.

"But I couldn't stop her could I?" she says pleadingly.

"How long has she known him?" Rita wants to know.

"A few months I suppose. She saw him at the shop where she works?"

"And where does he work?" Priya asks, thinking this may lead them to the pair.

"Yeh, well, there's a problem." Athena gesticulates wildly. "I went to Jed's flat - well I call it a flat, he just has – correction had - a room in a shared house. So a nice lad - Kevin or Calvin or something like that - answered the door and let me in. It was pretty chaotic, trousers on hangers suspended on door knobs,bean bags on the floor surrounded by dirty plates and pizza boxes, cans everywhere, a sign on a chalk board saying 'BILLS'. I couldn't see the sink for tea stains and heaven knows what else. Anyway," Athena shakes her head as she pulls herself away from the memory, "They said they hadn't seen Jed in well over a week. He'd gone and not left a contribution to the rent. So if I saw him would I remind him? Kevin – or was it Calvin- remembered Morwenna. She'd 'hung about a few nights' according to him, but he hadn't seen her for a while."

"So what did you do?" Priya asks cautiously, fearful that an angry and frustrated Athena may have acted out her fury on someone.

"What could I do? I asked him to let me know if Jed appeared and told him I'd do the same. Then I went to where he works – worked I should say!" Athena starts to pace the flat as she gets more agitated.

"Which is?" Rita interrupts,

"That bar in Market Street, what's it called, The Silver Shoe I think." Athena is gesticulating with her arms now as if showing the girls where the bar is.

Rita and Priya know Market Street, it is one of their favourite streets in Leicester and has two nail bars, as well as Fenwicks on the corner, a store in which they love to browse. But the bar they have not noticed. It's probably below ground or not obvious to shoppers passing by, Priya thinks.

"Well, Jed was a barman there. That's another reason I hated Morwenna hanging round him. Not just his age but he would work late, sometimes 'til 2, and she would hang out in the bar waiting for him. Goodness knows what sort of people she met there." Athena gives a shudder.

"So, of course, when I inquired – it took a while, the waitress at the bar didn't speak much English, she was Eastern European, but she fetched the assistant manager…" Athena pauses to sigh exasperatedly while she stares out of the flat's front window, which affords a little light but mostly a view of the steps leading up to the main part of the house.

"The manager said Jed had left, or just not turned up, about ten days ago. Just when Morwenna disappeared! He was paid cash in hand – it all sounded a bit dodgy to me - so he wasn't owed any wages. I guess he added to that with tips but even so it can't have been much, and for a man of that age to be living hand to mouth!" Athena shudders again.

"Do you have a phone number for him?" Rita asks "and what's his full name?" Priya wonders why she asks this; maybe her friend is thinking they might look for him on-line.

"Jed Chapman at least that's what he said, and I don't

think I do have a number." Athena picks up her phone and scrolls through her contacts.

"No. Nothing. How stupid of me! I should have asked!"

"Morwenna probably wouldn't have given it to you." Priya says reasonably as the girls drain their drinks.

"I'd better see to the guests." Athena tells them, collecting up the glasses and her undrunk cup of tea.

"Thanks for coming. It helps just to talk about it. I just don't know what else I can do!" she says exasperated. "She'll need to collect her A-level results next month. I don't know if she's going to uni or what…" her voice trails off.

"There's time for her to turn up before then." Rita says brightly, "Or she could take a gap year." she offers.

"It's not the end of the world. As long as she's safe." Priya stops, thinking that in her anxiety to stop Athena from worrying she is starting to sound like her own mother.

As the girls walk to the Peugeot they turn and wave to Athena who is standing on the steps which lead up to main the entrance to Sundial. "Try not to worry. We'll do what we can. She's a sensible girl." says Priya although she doesn't really think that. Morwenna has struck her as having her head in the clouds. The mystery is why such an obviously pretty girl, with an eye for fashion and the latest trends and labels, would want to hang around a man so much older than her with little money or status. Was she rebelling against her parents or was there more to it than that? Despite her reassuring words to Athena, Priya can see that Morwenna's life could be a whole lot more difficult if she does not come home and make some decisions about her future.

Rita presses her car key so the door unlocks to admit Priya, who climbs in and starts to looks at her phone to check out Morwenna and Jed on Facebook. She cannot find Jed and it's a while since Morwenna posted anything, which is unusual. Morwenna is one of those girls who collects 'likes' for things she has posted most days.

Meanwhile Rita gets behind the wheel and puts her phone on loudspeaker to play her phone messages. As the girls listen they hear the voice of Sergeant Griffiths. "Hello Rita." he says.

"Well I thought I'd better call." The Sergeant sounds reluctant to continue. 'Is there news about the DNA already, or are we in trouble?' thinks Priya.

"It's just that there's a couple of lads in A&E at the Infirmary. One of them won't let us call his parents, but I know who he is, see."

Rita and Priya look at each other, confused. "It's your younger brother, Rita, it's Nayan."

Chapter

12

"Anyone who sits on top of the largest hydrogen-oxygen fueled system in the world, knowing they're going to light the bottom, and doesn't get a little worried, does not fully understand the situation."

John Young, after being asked if
he was nervous about making the
first Space Shuttle flight in 1981.

Thursday, July 17th 2014 6.30pm

Arriving at the Infirmary, having parked in what has become her usual spot, Rita asks for her brother and is shown to a cubicle where Nayan sits on a bed, looking crushed and crumpled, as if the experience has knocked the spirit out of him. He holds his left arm awkwardly and there are sinister dark marks around his throat.

"Hi Rita!" he croaks, his voice lacking its usual force.

A female nurse appears before Rita can say anything, so she just waves sympathetically at her brother. Priya, standing behind her friend, tries to look reassuring, although she is shocked by Nayan's drooping appearance.

"Now then nothing broken just a sprain I'll bandage that up for you." the nurse says briskly, "The doctor says your neck will heal up, you may need to gargle with salt water for a few days to relieve your throat and paracetemol won't hurt for a day or two." The ginger haired nurse wraps his wrist expertly and swiftly in a bandage and then a sling.

"There, good to go." the nurse says. "We'll write to your GP but you shouldn't need a follow-up." She starts to tidy up the cubicle. "Boys will be boys" the nurse says to Rita as she vanishes back through the curtain.

"Well" Rita says, feeling like a living question mark. "What happened?"

"I need to check on Zeedan." Nayan evades as he slides off the bed one-handed, with Rita's help.

Back in the reception area of A&E they find Zeedan with his father who looks none too pleased.

"We just wanted to check you're okay." Nayan's friend says.

"Yeah." says Nayan.

"Have the police spoken to you?" Zeedan asks.

"Yeah." says Nayan.

"They have our addresses, they'll call if they need anything more." Zeedan adds.

"See you then." the boys exchange and Zeedan and his father exit through the automatic doors.

"Well?" Rita stands in front of her brother, her hands on her hips.

"It's no biggy." Nayan says, looking at the ground. "Some guys just attacked us."

"For no reason?" asks Priya, looking concerned.

"Yeh, we literally weren't doing anything. Just having a drink of Coke." Nayan explains, but the effort of speaking is clearly taking its toll on his throat.

"Like a drink now?" offers Rita, thinking of her brother's sore throat. "We can get you something in the café while Priya checks what's happening about her new nephew. Then you can come with me to the library, it's open late tonight."

Thursday, 17th July 2014 7.30pm

Rita, in the Central Library in Leicester, hopes some of Mohal's friends (he works there sometimes in the holidays) will be on duty and will help her access the online information from the registries about Michael and, more specifically, his brother Steven. How did he turn out a drug taker (if that's what he was?) who clearly kept bad company when Michael had turned out so well? she wonders, smiling across at Nayan who is sitting in the Sci-Fi section, a packet of throat sweets in his pocket. Priya has met up with her mother by the baby's cotside and will go home with her.

Around the library which, with its tiled floor and soaring ceiling, seems to have had grander ambitions for itself in the past, are stationed busts of famous men with quotations from their works: Francis Bacon, William Shakespeare and Lord Byron share this honour with John Locke and Isaac Newton. Nearby, the Town Hall clock chimes every 15 minutes reminding them they must soon go home and face the music.

Rita finds that the General Register Office keeps the Adopted Children Register which has details of adoptions authorised by court order since January 1927. The only information available is a certified copy of an entry which is the equivalent of a birth certificate for an adopted person. A full certificate has the date of the order and the name of the court as well as the particulars of the adoptive parents; the county, district and sub district are shown. The birth parents' names cannot be shown, she learns.

The certificate shows the child's adoptive name. To change a child's name a deed poll is needed, Rita finds. All these steps were taken for Michael to turn him from Michael Bailey to Michael Simmonds and are easy to trace in the records. Rita reads that the policy of Leicestershire County Council is not to support this sort of change (although the policy in the past may have been different and anyway the twins were covered by Birmingham Council). Leicestershire say the name (forename and surname) are a fundamental part of a child's history, culture and heritage. Rita hopes that Steven's name was not changed, that would make him easier to trace.

Rita's wish is granted. There is no adoption certificate for Steven Bailey. Now she is sad and regrets her wish. It looks possible that he never found a family and the sense of belonging which his brother clearly has.

Chapter

13

"I think it is likely that there is life out there. I fear we shall never know about it."

Richard Dawkins.

Saturday, 19th July 2014 7pm

"Nayan! Dinner is on the table!" Jahi shouts upstairs to his youngest child. The Patel family are gathering in Padma's state of the art kitchen, decked out in white wood units and grey slate work surfaces, for one her aromatic vegetable curries, the very smell of which acts like a pick-me-up. Padma has made a special effort to celebrate having Nayan home from A&E on Thursday with nothing more than a sore throat and a slightly hoarse voice to show for his escapade. She has waited for his sore throat to go down a little before arranging the meal.

For Mohal, Rita and Nayan the feast is a comforting reminder of home, for Jahi the meal is a sign that he married well. He likes his food and is copying his sons' example by starting to learn to cook a little himself. But he knows it will be a long while before he reaches even the lower slopes of the mountain of culinary perfection which his wife has climbed. They spoon the orange mixture onto their plates where it circulates like a moat around the carefully shaped mound of yellow speckled rice which Padma has positioned strategically on each warmed plate.Nayan and Mohal tear pieces of naan bread to dip into the vegetable sea. Jahi smiles with satisfaction at his family gathered together, Padma fusses about napkins and cutlery and tells the boys off for reaching across the table.

"Thank goodness nothing worse happened!" Padma says not for the first time. "I want you all well for the Balloon Experience trip in a couple of weeks." She reminds them of a post-exam treat she has organised for her younger two offspring.

"So where did you go today?" Rita wants to know of her younger brother.

She had again been brought to look out of her bedroom window earlier that day by a strange noise, and had witnessed her brother meeting his friend (the same boy that they saw at the Infirmary) by the lamp post in the street. This time the friend was riding a bike and the two had set off, quite dangerously, riding the bike together, Zeedan on the pedals and handle bars, Nayan on the seat.

"We hung out in the park a bit." Nayan admits between mouthfuls, recalling how he and Zeedan had propped the bike against the frame of the swings while they sat side by side, their long limbs causing their feet to scrape on the cushioned flooring provided by the council to reduce accidents. After checking briefly that neither was any the worse after the attack in Town Hall Square, they had talked about football.

"Can't wait for the season to start. City in the Premiership! We'll get Chelsea and Arsenal and all the other top clubs!" Nayan had been very excited the Saturday that Leicester City gained promotion and had shouted the news around the house as soon as it was announced and had tweeted about it.

They had talked about music, recalling the Kassabian concert at Victoria Park in Leicester that they had been lucky enough to attend in June, just as their GCSE exams were ending.

"Kassabian were so awesome!" Nayan was full of awe still.

"Respect." Zeedan agreed.

("Hello Leicester!" Tom Meighan, the lead singer, had said, "Can't believe we're in Vicky Park!" using the local term for the venue.)

Then the two boys had put their heads close together to watch on YouTube footage of various celebrities pouring buckets of ice water over their heads for charity.

"Crazy dudes!" they had laughed. Eventually their conversation, conducted as they swayed aimlessly backwards and forwards, had come round to the topic uppermost in Zeedan's mind.

"Momin is missing." Nayan blurts out now to his family, between mouthfuls of the curry.

"What do you mean?" asks his mother.

"His parents don't know where he is." Nayan adds.

Jahi shakes his head, "Oh no." he says and sucks his teeth thoughtfully.

"He's one of your mates?" Mohal checks.

"Yeah. It's all over Twitter and Facebook." Nayan continues, as if referring to social media makes the situation official.

"What's his full name?" Rita wants to know, thinking she can look him up online and see what she can find.

"Momin Ali" Nayan tells her. "Bit of a dickhead. Always showing off. He was in my drama group. He played Claudius."

Nayan's drama group had put on a production of Terry Pratchett's "Weird Sisters". Rita had been to see it. Not bad for Year 11 she had thought. She could vaguely recall the boy who played Claudius, a tall Asian boy who looked like he had started his growth spurt earlier than Nayan. Her younger brother had been a relatively late developer but was making up for it now, his arms and legs seemingly growing by the day ("You'll need new clothes for sixth form but we'll wait 'til August to buy them in case you grow some more." says Padma.)

"How come they don't know? The parents?" Padma says now, thinking that she would know where her children were, most of the time anyway, even Mohal at uni calls home frequently and they skype most weekends when he is away.

"They thought he was going to Cardiff, with his older

brother, to stay with their uncle, but he never arrived."

"I knew the brother I think." says Mohal, "He was a year below me at school." He speaks with a mouthful of the delicious curry mixture which earns him a critical look from his mother. "And no one knows where they are?" he continues, ignoring her glance.

"No. Zeedan says he heard about it at Mosque on Friday. Everyone was gossiping about it, speculating."

"Speculating?" Padma queries. "Speculating about what?"

"Oh, Ma, you know!" Nayan speaks as if it is obvious and reaches across the table for more naan, "Whether they've gone to Syria."

"To help the refugees you mean?" asks Mohal.

"No, more likely to fight. That's what everyone's saying."

"The brother was a bit of a hot head." Mohal confirms. "He was in the Cadet Force at school. I joined for a few weeks if you remember, but I soon left. I think Momin's brother was quite enthusiastic."

"Anyway it's not certain." Nayan clarifies, "But it's what everyone is saying."

"Their poor parents." Padma sympathises, "What a worry for them!"

"Would your friend know how to use a weapon? Was he in the cadets?" Mohal wants to know.

"Or who he's fighting for." puts in Jahi, drily.

"I don't think he's ever held a gun. He wasn't interested in the Cadets or anything, I literally don't think he's ever even slept outside, unlike his brother. The Cadets were always doing night hikes and sleeping under trees from what I've heard." Nayan tells his older brother.

"If they have gone, they'd be helping the refugees, wouldn't they?" Mohal tries again, hopefully. "The ones affected by the chemical weapons Assad is using against them, his own people. They'll be helping the rebels who we should have supported if the MPs hadn't voted against it last summer.

Man those refugees really need our help and we're doing nothing!" He reminds his family of where he stands on that issue, even though his views have brought him perilously close to trouble in the recent past.

"Well.", Jahi spreads his hands, resting them on his stomach after a plentiful supply of the curry, "I think it may be more complicated than that. I expect Momin belongs to a Sunni mosque - most of them are?"

"Don't know." says Nayan, "We talk about science and cricket mostly."

"Mmmn. Well as far as I have heard the Mosques here are very strict, very orthodox and closer to the ideas of the Taliban than you might think. Most of them are Sunni I think. The Sunnis seem to be fighting the Shias now, so I guess if your friend has gone to Syria or Iraq he will be caught up in that." says Jahi shaking his head again. "What do they call themselves? ISIS, I think. They seem to be a ruthless and dangerous group. I do hope he is not with them."

For once Nayan stops eating, thinking about his friend and how he may be risking his life abroad.

"Let me get this straight." says Mohal with a cheeky grin on his face. "Your friend Momin is missing (pointing at his brother), your friend Morwenna is missing and Mr Gregson's friend Maureen is missing?" (pointing at his sister). "Well surely you see the connection?" he pauses. The family look satisfyingly confused.

"They all have names beginning with 'M'! Perhaps aliens are taking them! Keep an eye on me, I could be next!" he grins.

Rita shakes her head at his nonsense and Nayan throws his napkin at Mohal across the table.

"Ha ha not." says the younger brother sarcastically, helping himself to a large slice of the pineapple which Padma has now supplied.

"Well here's another theory then." Mohal is undeterred.

"What if they've gone with that missing plane?"

"The Malaysian Airlines one you mean? The one they haven't found yet?" says Nayan who seems to be giving the idea some thought.

"Exactly. Spooky innit?" Mohal puts on a scary voice.

"Let's be sensible for a moment" says Jahi trying to restore order at the table. "Tell us again how you got attacked in the town centre."

Nayan shrugs. "I dunno really." he starts. "Me and Zeedan" (Jahi restrains himself from correcting his son's grammar) "We were just hanging. We took the bike round the Market and then put it by a bench in the square so's we could drink a Coke."

"And then?" Jahi presses.

"There were these weirdos on the other side of the Square." Nayan tells him.

"Weirdos?" Rita queries.

"Yeh, you know, black jackets or coats, helmets, there were quite a few of them hanging around." Nayan says.

"Bikers?" this from Mohal.

"I guess. We didn't like the looks they were giving us so we were going to split. Only before we could move they came over and started shouting. One of them pushed Zeedan to the ground, another got hold of my throat." Nayan rubs at his neck at the memory.

"Lucky that policeman was around!" says Padma who has taken fruit and flowers to the temple already in gratitude for her son's escape.

(Rita thinks to herself that the presence of the police may not have been fortuitous. Wasn't it Town Hall Square where Michael had been stabbed? The police probably had the area under surveillance. She decides to say nothing, not wanting to alarm her parents further.)

"I guess." says Nayan who feels there would have been less fuss if the policeman had not been there. He and Zeedan would have gone home and not said anything. As it was, everyone was making a big deal of it.

"Well from now on, I don't want you hanging about in any parks or open spaces." says Jahi. "You hear far too many stories of people being beaten up for all sorts of reasons. If you need to get anywhere either your mother or I, or your brother or sister,will take you and fetch you."

The table falls silent. Padma and Jahi are pondering what else might have happened but for the intervention of the police; Nayan is sullenly envisaging a curtailment to his freedom; Rita and Mohal are thinking they had not passed their driving tests to babysit their younger brother!

Saturday, 19th July 2014 9pm

"Is that him?" Rita asks.

"It's hard to tell" says Nayan.

Brother and sister stare hard at the YouTube image they have frozen on the screen. The picture shows 5 men, sitting in a semicircle, wearing khaki clothes with traditional Arab scarves (a shemagh or keffiyeh) wrapped round their shoulders and the lower part of their faces, the background is a desert scene straight from *Homeland*. The surroundings are as anonymous and unidentifiable, threatening and treacherous in their empty vastness, as the armed men seated on the ground.

"It might be Momin, his fringe always stuck up a bit like that." Nayan says.

"But surely he'll have changed since he joined them? They all look the same to me." observes Rita.The picture seems posed to her. Like when you go for a novelty photo at a studio and stand in front of a Victorian scene; it is as if the fighters have gone back to a time when sepia was the only colour.

"He's an idiot if it is him!" says Nayan "He'll never get good A-levels now."

"I think that's the least of his problems." Rita replies. "He surely doesn't think he'll be able to resume his studies here, even if he survives? Who would have him? It's not great for your CV is it? What did you do in your gap year - oh I killed a few fellow Muslims, decapitated some Christians, in order to bring in the caliphate!"

"Well his tweet says it's him. Second from the right." Nayan tells Rita.

"And he's definitely with ISIS?" Rita is still incredulous.

"So he says." Nayan confirms "Religion is crazy, isn't it?" he adds.

"I don't think it's really about religion," says Rita, "From what I've read – Salman Rushdie has written on the subject - from what I understand him to say, both Muslim factions - the Shias and the Sunnis - mangle the language to make it look as though the fight is about religion when it's not at all, it's about power. Both sets of extremists see modernity as the enemy, especially with its language of liberty for women and its emphasis on legitimate government rather than tyranny. I think Rushdie says young people are attracted by 'Jihadi cool' – the deformed medievalist language of fanaticism backed up by modern weaponry. That's what your friend has fallen for. It is a hate-filled rhetoric appealing to angry young men. Most people who suffer under the new Islamic fundamentalism are other Muslims. If only people didn't think they had to be right!" finishes Rita. "Isn't tolerating other people and their beliefs more important?"

Nayan is taken aback by his sister's vehemence. "I thought I'd go to the Space Centre tomorrow." he says, changing the subject. "Can you pick me up?" he asks.

Chapter

14

"When the moon is ninety degrees away from the sun it sees but half the earth illuminated (the western half). For the other (the eastern half) is enveloped in night. Hence the moon itself is illuminated less brightly from the earth, and as a result its secondary light appears fainter to us."

Gallileo Gallilei

Wednesday, 23rd July 2014 3pm

In the Infirmary after her attack, when Rita starts to wake from her morphine dreams she is unsure where she is. She knows it is the hospital, but she feels as if in the course of her stay she has been moved around the building (this is not in fact the case as she comes to realise when her mind starts to settle). Has she really been here in the same bed all the time?

A face she recognises and one she doesn't are looking at her.

"Hello, Rita, you look a bit better." Her mother is standing by her, arranging some cards – presumably with 'get well' wishes - that are on the cabinet which stands next to her bed.

"How do you feel?" asks the other Asian woman, who has shoulder length hair in a crisp bob and whose stethoscope indicates she is a doctor.

"Okay." says Rita who has not really decided yet how she feels.

"We'll just do some tests." And the doctor proceeds to put Rita through her paces while she scrutinises the results; Rita finds herself pushing against the doctor with her hands, touching her own nose with her fingers, locking her fingers together, grinning, and then crossing her arms. The doctor takes a rubber hammer and bangs it against her knees to test her reactions and she scrapes a pen along the soles of Rita's feet.

"Good." the doctor pronounces. Then she says "You remember what happened to you?" and Rita reaches into her brain for the information and finds… nothing.

"I'm not sure." she says, puzzled, looking round for a drink of water to buy time.

Her mother, concern lining her forehead, pours Rita a glass and looks from doctor to daughter and back again.

"Not to worry." the young doctor says, standing up to go. "You've had a nasty knock on the head. It can take a while for your memory to come back fully. There's plenty of time. I'll call back tomorrow."

"That's it?" says Padma, "Wait and see?"

The doctor pauses on the threshold of the room. "Rest and not worrying will be the best medicine" she says to mother and daughter, "Don't stress about it. But if you want to do something, try keeping a diary or a blog. Some people find writing about what they can remember helps them recall other things." and then she is gone.

"The doctor is right, you should rest." says Padma as Rita pulls a face at the back of the retreating medic. She is finding this situation frustrating.

"All right." she says to please her mother, "But can Priya come and see me? I'm sure she'll help me unlock some memories."

Padma nods and soon Rita, despite herself, is dozing again.

Wednesday, 23rd July 2014 7pm

After attempting an unappetising meal, Rita drifts off and is woken half an hour later by the scraping sound of a chair being moved as her friend Priya settles by her side.

"Am I glad to see you!" says Rita, sitting up and checking there is no one else in the room. "Mum is so stressed, she's driving me crazy!"

"She only wants you to get better." Priya reassures. "She told me not to get you over-tired." she goes on "She was like, 'Rita's very unwell, you know, and needs to rest, that's what the doctors say.'"

"As if!" says Rita exasperated.

"Yeh, well, I don't mind" Priya shrugs her shoulders.

"So can you?" Rita asks.

"Can I what?" Priya is puzzled.

"Tell me things that might get my brain going again." Rita explains.

"Oh, I'm not sure I should." Priya hesitates, fearing she will get the blame if it makes Rita worse.

"Come on!" Rita urges "Try me with something."

"Well, you know your name and mine." Priya begins.

"Yeah, yeah."

"And your family and where you live."

"10 Elm Drive" Rita recites like a mantra. "It's recent stuff I don't know. Like how I got here."

"By ambulance I think." Priya jokes.

"Ha, ha, you're hilarious." Rita pretends to grin, then recalls that was one of the tests the doctor did and slowly lets the smile fade in case it betrays some kind of abnormality.

"I don't think we should talk about what happened." Priya tells her, "But how about telling me some history? You're fond of that!" Priya encourages.

"Cool beans. It might work I guess." says Rita, thinking that using one part of her memory might prompt another to come to life.

"Pass me my iPad." she asks, then, "What bit of history?" she asks Priya.

"Well, you said you were really getting into the Wars

of the Roses, because of Richard III and all that." she says hesitantly, looking carefully at Rita's face in case this is the wrong thing to say.

"Oh yeah!" Rita settles her head on her pillows and taps on the iPad to look up her notes before making herself comfortable for her discourse.

"So it all kicked off in 1455 and went on for 30 years." she begins.

"That's a long time!" Priya says, reaching in her bag for her comb.

"Well, they weren't fighting all the time. There were truces and periods of quiet in between. Then it would flare up again."

"What flared up? What was it all about and where does Richard come in?" Priya asks, passing the comb through her ponytail.

"He was at the end, of course. His death meant the end of the Plantagenets as kings and the start of the Tudors." Rita explains "The House of Plantagenet started to rule in 1154 with Henry II, although they were first known under their French name of Anjou or Angevin."

"So why Plantagenets? It's a strange name?" Priya queries.

"It was probably a nickname that stuck. Something to do with a plant – broom it's called – and maybe one of them used to wear it or plant it." Rita shrugs, "Some member of the family may have used it to show they were of old stock, in contrast to new people who were being given titles. Whatever, things started to go wrong with the death of the Black Prince."

"He sounds interesting!" says Priya, "Why was he called that?"

Rita looks it up. "Mmmn. Seems it was only later, long after he was dead, that the term was widely used; they think it was what the French called him at Battle of Crecy, on account of his black armour. He was really called Edward."

"Another one!" Priya exclaims, "Why do they have to

have the same name? It's very confusing!" She gets a critical look from her friend.

"The Black Prince was the eldest son of Edward III. He was born in Woodstock near Oxford." Rita continues. "He was good at fighting, as you might imagine with that name, and he had successes fighting against France in the Hundred Years War.Anyway, he fell ill in France, died at Westminster in 1376 aged 45 and is buried in Canterbury. It meant that when Edward III died a year later the throne passed to the son of the Black Prince, Richard. Edward III had lots of children, including five sons. Later on, when all the arguments started and various people made claims to the throne, most of them could trace their claim back to him."

"Richard was only 10 years old when he became Richard II. Parliament and various advisers ruled while he was a child, obv."

"Obv." says Priya, not convinced it is as obvious as her friend suggests.

"When Richard was 14 he dealt with the Peasants Revolt." Rita goes on.

"Oh dear." says Priya, not sure what that was.

"This was in 1381." Rita helps her out, "An army of peasants marched on London and captured the Tower! They were unhappy about the taxes at a time when they were struggling to feed their families, especially the poll tax." Rita fills in.

"Well I've heard of that." Priya interjects.

"So Richard met the rebels in London at Mile End. The rebel leader, Wat Tyler, was killed, but Richard made the peasants promises which made them go away. Of course he didn't keep them. But his success went to his head a bit. Richard thought he was better than he was. He was a good patron of the arts, but he was rather overstrung and fastidious; he even invented the pocket handerkerchief!"

"No! He sounds well gay!" Priya gives her opinion.

"He may have been inclined that way," Rita agrees, "Richard chose favourites who he was rumoured to sleep with. He made high-handed and arbitrary decisions which alienated lots of people. His big mistake was to banish an opponent, Henry Bolingbroke, who was his cousin, the son of a powerful nobleman called John of Gaunt, who was Richard's uncle and the third son of Edward III."

"And was he?" Priya asks.

"Was he what?" Rita is puzzled.

"Gaunt. Was he a thin man?" Priya queries.

"I think he was, yeah." Rita says looking quizzically at Priya. "Actually, it says here he died in Leicester Castle!"

"Never! Where is the castle again?" Priya has to ask.

"It's the County Court in the centre of town, near St Nicholas Circle.There's been a castle on the site since the Norman conquest, it says here, and the Great Hall was even used by Parliament in the past.Beside the Hall is a building known as the dungeon or John of Gaunt's cellar." Rita recites from the castle website.

"Creepy." says Priya, not sure how any of this is getting them to the Wars of the Roses.

"Well, this is the interesting bit." Rita warms to her theme. "All through the Plantagenets the succession had been followed. Sons or grandsons. No argument. But then Henry Bolingbroke broke with all that and deposed Richard II. It was a popular move. But it set a precedent. It showed that bad kings could be replaced, and when the disputes started it showed that the side that won could claim the throne even if they didn't have the best right of succession."

"Uhuh." Priya is thoughtful.

"So, although there were better claims to the throne, Henry, who was from the House of Lancaster, held on to it and passed the throne to his son, Henry V.He married the daughter of the King of France and his son, Henry VI, is the only one to have been crowned both King of England and of

France. Henry VI was a baby when he became king –"

"No way!" Priya interrupts, Rita gives her another warning look and continues,

"And England and Wales were ruled by his uncles."

"So that's what the wars were about? Who should be king?" Priya is beginning to see now.

"More or less. It was about rich families, really, and choosing which side you thought would win." Rita acknowledges.

"Like choosing teams in the Apprentice?" Priya imagines the situation,

"Sort of." Rita half agrees, "Some families had sworn to help others; some hoped for riches or positions. And some people changed sides. The biggest question mark was over the Stanley family, whose intervention was decisive at the Battle of Bosworth, but we're getting ahead of ourselves. Pass me some water would you?" Rita asks, clearing her throat.

Priya looks at her friend to check she is not getting too tired, but in fact Rita seems animated, and more like her old self, so she encourages her to continue when she has her drink.

"So it began in 1455?" she reminds Rita.

"Yeh." Rita sips the water, "With the first battle of St Albans." Rita is checking her iPad for details.

"Really?" Priya is surprised "You've been there haven't you? It's near Mohal's uni?" She checks.

"Yeah, that's right. We went to look at the Abbey there. Well there were two battles in St Albans in the Wars of the Roses in fact. The second one was in 1461."

"Who was the King when it started and why is it called Wars of the Roses?" Priya asks.

"Henry VI was the king. He seems to have had some mental illness which didn't help to keep the country together. The Richard who started it all was Duke of York and the Yorkist emblem was a white rose. The other side were Lancastrians and their symbol was a red rose." Rita explains.

"Bit mad isn't it?" says Priya

"I guess it's not unlike rival gangs today arguing about postcodes. It makes about as much sense." Rita replies, "Generations were involved. Fathers got killed on the battlefield and sons carried on. Henry VI wasn't very popular, largely because of his advisers, and, like I said, he had some mental instability. It must have been a huge contrast with his father, Henry V, who was a strong fighting king, you know, the one that won the battle of Agincourt."

"So what happened at the first battle of St Albans?" Priya wants to know.

"Richard Duke of York was marching south towards London and his forces were on the Ermine Road – the old Roman Road which goes through St Albans. The two sides clashed in the market place in the town." Rita tells her.

"Really? In the middle of St Albans?" Priya checks "It seems such a quiet place from what you've said."

"There was fighting in the streets but the battle didn't last long; somewhere between 60 and 100 men were killed, which isn't many really." Rita goes on, "There is a plaque on the site where the Castle Inn was;it records that Edmund Beaufort, 2nd Duke of Somerset, one of the King's men, was killed there. After the battle, Richard met up with the King, but it was pretty clear the issues weren't settled and that both sides were gearing up for another fight, which happened at Blore Heath in Cheshire in 1459."

Priya smiles to herself. Nothing wrong with Rita's brain as she reels off these battle locations and dates!

"This was a major battle on open ground, not like the skirmish in St Albans. It showed the country was in the throes of a proper civil war. The battle ebbed and flowed, but eventually the Yorkists got the upper hand and some of the Lancastrians swapped sides while others retreated quickly towards Market Drayton. About 3,000 men died in that battle."

"Wow." says Priya, laying down her comb, "The casualties were mounting up!"

"You bet. I guess that makes people more determined in a way. They would want to avenge earlier deaths. Anyway, the Lancastrians won at Ludford Bridge in 1459 but the Yorkists gained the upper hand in 1460 at the battle of Northampton after the Earl of Warwick arrived on the scene from France to help Richard of York."

"Warwick, I've heard of him haven't I?" Priya feels a memory stirring.

"Yeah. I'm going to do a project on him when I get to uni." Rita says confidently. Then she continues, "In the same year, 1460, there was another battle, at Wakefield; this was won by the Lancastrians and Richard of York was killed."

"So he's not our Richard?" Priya checks she is following all this.

"No, he is his father. His sons included Edward who became Edward IV, George, Duke of Clarence, the one who drowned in a barrel of wine so they say, and Richard III. The battle of St Albans kicked off in 1461. Warwick was camped around the north of the city with about 9,000 Yorkists while around 12,000 Lancastrians marched south towards London from Wakefield. Edward, Richard of York's eldest son, should have joined up with Warwick but was busy on the Welsh border beating the Lancastrians, led by Owen Tudor and Jasper Tudor, at the battle of Mortimor's Cross."

"This is the second battle of St Albans?" Priya checking again.

"Yes, that's right. The armies met on Barnard's Heath and Nomansland Common. The Yorkists had set up various defences around the town, but the attack did not come in the direction the Yorkists had anticipated, probably because they were betrayed by Sir Henry Lovelace whom the Lancastrians had captured at Wakefield. Warwick was slow to realise the main attack was happening on Barnards Heath and by the time he sent extra forces along the Sandridge Road it was too late, and by evening the Yorkists retreated to Chipping Norton. They think the Lancastrians lost about 2,000 men in the second battle of St Albans and the Yorkists about 4,000."

"That's a lot!" Priya says.

"Yeah, it's one of those battles that gets re-enacted, as the Heath still exists, but they don't have the numbers of course. In fact in 2011 there was a conference there to commemorate the 550th anniversary." Rita tells her friend.

"After that the Yorkists had nearly all the successes, including the battle of Towton in Yorkshire in 1461." she goes on, "Edward and Warwick were able to join together in London and Edward was declared King. But by 1469 Warwick and Edward had become enemies. For one thing Warwick wanted him to marry a French noble woman but Edward spoiled that by marrying Elizabeth Woodville."

"Oh yeah, I've seen a programme about her." Priya remembers.

"Warwick restored Henry VI, the deposed Lancastrian king, to the throne. Then Edward routed Warwick at the battle of Barnet and Warwick was killed. Henry VI died in 1471 and Edward IV in 1483 after which our Richard took over from Edward's son."

"The princes in the tower." Priya reminds herself.

"Exactly. Lots of theories about that. Anyway, Bosworth was in 1485, as you know," Rita says and Priya nods as if she does know, "There was one more battle after Bosworth, at Stoke in 1487, but it was all over by then really. Richard III was beaten by Henry at Bosworth and he became Henry VII, using the Tudor name from his father, Edmund Tudor. Henry married the daughter of Edward IV and Elizabeth Woodville and combined the red and white roses into the Tudor emblem. And things settled down for a while."

"I think you should settle down now and get some sleep."

says Priya. "You've covered a lot of ground."

"Yeah." says Rita "But it's really helped. I'm going to use my iPad next… I'm going to start a blog to see if it will help unblock my memory."

Chapter

15

GIRL SEEKS SELF

By Rita

Thursday, 24th July 2014 10am

I am starting this journal 2day to help me remember, to find myself, I guess.

My name is Rita Patel BTW. I am eighteen years old and I live in Leicester. I'm posting a selfie so you can see what I look like.

How did I get lost? Well that's the big question, my memory is not so good. DBEYR! Before I get to that there are questions I may be able to answer.

Where am I? I am lying on a bed on the fourth floor of Leicester Royal Infirmary. I am lucky enough to have a room of my own but that may change if I continue to get better! They may move me to a general ward or they may let me go home. Don't know which I would prefer. A ward would not be v. comfy & I wldn't have my things round me. But home means my parents fussing, especially my mother, and that can be very tiring!

So I am not technically lost? Well, no. It's bits of my memory I've mislaid after an accident and I want to use this blog to help me find them again.

So I know I have a family? Well yeah, of course I know I have a mum and a dad and a brother – no, wait, I have two brothers. And I know I am lucky because not everybody knows what family they come from or lives with their birth parents, which is odd. Why do I know that? Who has told me that?

Food for thought later.

Talking of food, here's a picture of the lunch they just brought me. Not great is it? Mostly breadcrumbs (again I feel someone said that to me but who could it have been?)-potato croquettes and grated cheese, apple crumble floating in a pale liquid.

Here's 3 things I like about being in hospital –

People make a fuss of you and bring you nice things (I'll post pics of the chocs and PJs I've been given!)

Your parents don't nag you to do stuff or tell you off. It's a great 'get out of jail free' card.

It's quiet so I get to sleep when I want to, which is quite a lot at the moment. I'm like a baby! (Funny that - I think I know about a baby-wonder what baby that is?)

Here's 3 things I don't like about being in hospital –

(1) They wake you up so early! It's when the new shift take over I guess but it's way too soon. I thought sick people were meant to rest!

(2) Strangers come into my room all the time. Unless you ask, they don't always tell you who they are or what they're doing. How'm I supposed to know? One guy was checking the smoke alarm, then there's the cleaners (who are lovely BTW), caterers, health care assistants (they help you to wash and go to the bathroom if you need it) porters, nurses, doctors, occupational therapists, hospital volunteers – mine's a cheery lady called Cherry who puts her head round my door to see if I want her to buy anything from the hospital shop. Really, all those people in and out and none of them knows what the others have said or done, I keep on having to tell them.Grays Anatomy it isn't!

(3) The food. I've blogged about this before. I checked and the Infirmary is 1,053rd out of 1,258 hospitals in the country, so that explains a lot! How difficult is it to put together a decent macaroni cheese? Or a vegetable bake? I think they should get back to basics, start with easy things that everyone can eat. People don't want gourmet food ideas just meals that are simple

and sustaining. And what if every ward had a microwave? Then at least you could heat up your meal if it arrives a bit cold. Or sometimes the medics want to do annoying things just when the dinner trolley arrives – like they take you for a scan - and then the food's stone cold when you get back. I'm just going to order sandwiches from now on. They might not be very exciting but there's not much they can do wrong with them!

Girls seeks self
By Rita

Thursday, 24th July 2014 5pm

I slept most of the day. Shaming isn't it? Can't decide if it's because I'm ill or bored.

When can I go home?

I think that's what I want now. I'm starting to be afraid my memory won't come back while I'm in this artificial atmosphere. May be if I'm at home in my room it will jog my brain? Hey. It's got to be worth a try!

Girl seeks self
By Rita

Friday, 25th July 2014 9am

Home today! I'm v. excited but also a bit scared. What if I get ill, pass out or something when I get there? How will mum and dad cope?

Also, what if it's noisy – I expect the boys will be playing their music and having their loud friends round.

Add to which, what if I still don't remember what happened?

11am

Still waiting to go home. You can't just walk out or check out like in a hotel.

You have to –

1. *be discharged by the doctor*
2. *have the agreement of the occupational therapist (or 'terrorist' as I call her, she's a scary woman with grey hair that looks like she irons it and she wears round glasses and she looks at you intently. She's like a character from a Roald Dahl book, what were those Aunts in James and the Giant Peach? Aunt Sponge and Aunt Spiker). (Oh look, see what I done there - I'm remembering something random! Maybe more things will come back to me!)*
3. *have your TTAs – that's the medication they want you to take home. So you have to wait for the pharmacy to send the pills up to the ward. Every time the messenger arrives with a few packages you hope it's yours but there's no way of knowing. You just have to wait.*

2.30pm

Hurrah! The nurse says my TTAs are on the trolley which is making its way up here. My brother, Mohal, has come to fetch me as my parents are working at their dental practice (I remember all that, see!). Mohal is sitting beside me now, playing Candy Crush, so much for his bedside manner! Dr House watch out!

4.30pm

Great relief to be home (I think). I remember the house and where my room is. I remember where I keep things – this is good news!

The downside is I felt a bit shaky and nauseous (sorry to bring that up, if you see what I mean!) on the journey. The car seemed to be moving so fast! It wasn't Mohal's driving (which is quite good TBH). I just haven't been anywhere (except the bathroom!) for a while and it all got a bit much.

"You're not going to throw up are you?" Mohal kept asking me in the car, which frankly wasn't helping. (Apologies if this is TMI) "Keep looking out of the window, at the horizon." he said, as if I was sea sick!

When we got to a set of traffic lights he said "Do you want to get out? Get some air?" but I thought that would be worse so I gritted my teeth and crossed my fingers (the brain doctor would be pleased, I can do both at the same time!).

I lay on my bed when we got back – my pink duvet – until the dizziness went away. Nayan – my other brother, he's younger than me- came in to check I was ok and brought me some orange juice. As he bent over me and said "Rita, are you all right?" I had half a memory. I'm sure I've heard him say that before. But when? It's tantalising.

There's no point trying too hard. That's what the doctor said. The memories will rise to the surface of my mind when they are ready like corks in a bowl of water - LOL!

I fell asleep after Nayan had gone. Just half an hour and I feel much better, my head is clearer. I'm going to do the whole of Twilight I've decided. The box set. If I drop off I can watch from where I fell asleep.I do love Robert Pattinson and the whole vampire thing! It's sooooo cool!

Guess what, I'd just started Twilight (the first one's called 'Twilight 'natch! -in case you don't know!) when my BFF, Priya, turned up (change that, BFFTTEE!) . Her mum came too, just to say "hi" and see how I was, then she went off to do something. They had brought some vegetable samosas – delicious! Just what I fancied. Priya nibbled at hers but I gobbled mine! That's what hospital food does for you!

Priya says it's weird I can't remember what happened.Here's what she asked me-

"What's your most recent memory?"

(That's easy- eating the samosa!)

No, she didn't mean that. She meant before my 'accident'.

How do I know? How do I know what order things occurred in? What came before what? And lots of things are only impressions or sensations. My mind has imprints in it like those left by dreams you can't quite remember. They leave you with a feeling, but you can't describe rationally what happened in the dream.

"OK" she said "so you know your name"

-Of course, duh!

"And you know your family?"

"Yeah, yeah!"

"And school, you remember our school?"

And that did the trick, Good for Priya! She'll make a great doctor one day (I know that's what she wants to be, she told me).

Suddenly in my mind's eye I could see fingers touching, Priya's and someone else's. A boy was handing Priya a drink in a glass. The room was dark but there were lights circling around it. Where were we? Music was playing. There were lots of people dancing and laughing around us. It was the school Prom! I wore my turquoise shalwar kamiz and Priya had a yellow sari. Her friend, who gave her the drink, is Ben, Ben Cohen. I remember now! They're going out together! He's well fit! Lucky Priya! I'm pleased for her, but he does take up a lot of her time, she's always on the phone to him when she comes to see me, or texting or messaging.

But hey, things are going to change aren't they? We have to move away to go to uni. I hope she and I will always be friends though. The Prom was because we've done our A-levels (good job my accident was after the exams, what if I'd forgotten all that stuff before I sat them? I might not have been able to go to uni!)

I got so excited at all the things I could remember about the Prom that I think Priya got scared I was overdoing it, so she left, which was a bore as I really felt I was making progress. Come back soon I said and she said may be Meera will come with the baby, he's out of hospital now!

As I drifted off into one of my naps (Robert will have to wait) I could hear Priya and Mohal talking about me in the kitchen in subdued voices.

3 good things about being ill –
1. *People are nice to you*
2. *You don't have to help around the house*
3. *You can eat what you like (I had ice cream for breakfast!!!)*

3 bad things about being ill –
1. *People talk about you, sometimes when you're in the room ("She looks hot/cold. Does she need a drink? Would she like some books or magazines?" Hello! I am here you know!)*
2. *You can't do what you want. I remember that I was planning to redecorate my room – I found the sites I was looking at on my iPad – but I'm not allowed out of the house according to my parents, let alone allowed to go buying paint and start using it!*
3. *Relatives keep visitng. Aunt Jaina came today with my identical twin cousins Shona and Shreya. They are 14, two years younger than Nayan and from the planet 'super well behaved'! I doubt they'd recognise a normal teenage tantrum if they saw one! They were in matching dresses and sandals and their long black hair was in plaits which must have taken them hours! Maybe they sit and do each other's hair? It must be like looking at yourself in the mirror? Anyway I would prefer not to have them intruding in my bedroom – this is my space – but mum won't let me go downstairs yet ("You mustn't over do it") so there was no choice. From the look on her face, Jaina did not approve of the Twilight DVDs which were strewn on the floor (She should see*

what the boys watch!)Her girls (my cousins, I guess) have been watching a box set of Jane Austen's novels apparently (whoopidoo!) and they asked me which was my favourite. The only one I could remember was Pride and Prejudice – that scene with Colin Firth in the lake that makes my mum go weak at the knees – so I said that to shut them up!

A good thing about being ill (I know, I've added another one) is you can ask people to leave by saying you don't feel well or you need to rest. So after 10 minutes of hearing about Shona and Shreya's archery course at the County cricket ground, and Jaina's suggestions for getting rid of a headache, I pretended to feel a bit weak and Mum showed them out. Then of course they started talking about me! I must insist I can leave my bedroom tomorrow, then maybe I can get out of the house and back to normal!

Girl seeks self
By Rita

Saturday, 26th July 2014 11am

I woke in the night after a bad dream. Well it wasn't bad so much as weird and here's what it was as best I can describe. I was in a house, I didn't recognise it at first. But one of the problems with identifying it was that the rooms - or at least the room I was in - was full of grey swirling clouds. Like I was in the sky or something. After a bit I realised from the acrid smell that the clouds were actually smoke! And also I realised that there was an insistent beeping noise which must have been a smoke alarm. Now, in my dream, I was frightened. Where was the fire? How could I escape? Could I put out the fire perhaps? The smoke was getting greyer and thicker, it was catching in my throat and I was starting to choke. That's when I woke up and found I was coughing. I checked my phone for messages-

one from Priya about coming round. Sitting up in bed, though, the idea of the dream, the sensation, the feeling wouldn't go away and suddenly I remembered!

"Meera's baby" Priya had said. I remembered the day, the evening; we (Priya and I) got back to Priya's house and there was her mother all agitated because her sister was at the hospital having the baby. And it was coming early. Imagine! I remembered all that! And there's more. Next thing was that Priya went into the house and I followed – well I overtook them TBH, because I could hear the smoke alarm and I could smell smoke. I followed the beeping noise to the kitchen and found that Mrs Shah had left a pan on the hob which had boiled dry and it was starting to burn.

I moved the pan to the sink and poured water on it, then turned off the the hob and opened all the windows I could find to encourage the smoke to go, while closing the kitchen door to stop it spreading down the hall. That was when Priya came in with the news that Meera had had a boy, and danced me down the hall and back and I made everyone tea, because that's what they do on Call the Midwife.

Now I want to talk to Priya ASAP. She seems able to help me unlock my memory. Maybe she can help some more!

Girl seeks self
By Rita

Friday, 25th July 2014 (contd.)

Priya came round today and I did make it downstairs. I'm going to go out tomorrow. I don't care what anyone says, the new King Richard III Centre is open and I want to go!!! That can't do any harm can it?

We watched the first Hunger Games – that's my favourite - I <u>so</u> want to be Katniss Everdeen! I'm trying to train my hair to hang down at the front like hers does, but mine's too curly! And Priya tried me with various names ("Do you think that's a good *idea?""" Mum said. Well how else am I going to remember?)*

So while we watched the film Priya said to me-

"Mr Gregson"

And I said "That's easy, he's in the care home in Thurmaston. He helped me with my history projects. He lived next door to us when I was little."

"And recently? Have we been to see him in the last couple of weeks?" she continued her interrogation

But I had nothing. That was disappointing.

We drank our J20s and ate Doritos.

Then Priya said-

"Michael"

And I said "Missing" and she's like "What do you mean "Missing?" and I'm like "Morwenna is missing" and Priya said "Yes that's right but I didn't say Morwenna" and I said "People are missing, like that Malaysian airliner" and Nayan (who'd come in by then to find out what I was getting excited about) said "What do you know about an airliner?" and I said (I said! I remembered so clearly! Weird!) "You know the plane that disappeared, the one they can't find, not the one that crashed in the Ukraine, that was another one," and you should have seen the look on their faces! They were amazed I could recall so much.

So then I thought I should write it all down and that maybe that would jog my memory some more.

So I decided to write more lists –

Here we go-

LIST ONE

What I know I know

- *I know lots of things now.*
- *My favourite colour is turquoise - so deep like the sea*
- *My favourite singer is George Ezra – deep voice!*
- *My favourite subject is History – so deep, endlessly interesting*

- *My favourite film is Frozen I want to go to a singalong showing. So cute! ("Let it go! Let it go! Let it go!")*

What else?

(1) Morwenna is missing, Priya and I saw Athena, her mother, who says she has probably run off with her boyfriend. Morwenna's not my mate, she's not my kind of girl but I like Athena so I'm worried on her behalf. Priya says Morwenna hasn't tweeted or put anything on Facebook for ages, which just isn't like her. You'd think she'd be boasting about the boyfriend and trying to get likes for him.

(2) Mr Gregson asked for help. He has lost – he has lost his friend! I remember now- Mable? Mathilda? Maureen! That's it! Maureen Cummings. She went missing after a visit to the Space Centre, which …

Girl seeks self
By Rita

Friday, 25th July 2014 (contd, contd.)

Sorry, brain overload! So many ideas came into my head when I wrote 'Space Centre', it's as if there isn't room for them all. It was like falling to earth really fast (like that space mascot they sent into orbit! I remember that!), all the info coming rushing towards me, like too much traffic getting jammed in the rush hour at the M1/M69 junction.

I must make sense of this. I've got Cummmings/Steve/Michael/Post Mortem/ Code.

Are these things I know or don't know?

Come with me through the maze and let's find out. Oh- and Nayan getting attacked, and me getting… oh yes, now I know what happened to me! OMG it's like starting an avalanche! Can't wait to talk to Priya again.

OK, so here goes. I'm going to do a timeline because I think it will help me to remember what order things happened in.

Wot you have to remember is that Priya and me saw a busker in Birmingham who we think is related to the dead man she saw in a post-mortem examination. The busker turned out to be called Michael and he told us he had a brother called Steve.Now read on…..

<u>*Here's the timeline-*</u>
- *July 1 Mr Gregson's Care Home visited the Space Centre*
- *July 1 'Steve' (probably) was killed*
- *July 2 'Steve's' body was found at the Space Centre*
- *July 3 Priya and Ben (!) went to a Post- Mortem on 'Steve'*
- *July 3 Morwenna left home & went missing*
- *July 3 Nayan went to the Space Centre and couldn't get in because of the police*
- *July 12 Maureen left the Care Home and went missing*
- *July 13 Michael was stabbed in Town Hall Square – I mean he was in the Square when he was stabbed, silly! His wound is in his stomach and just missed his kidneys.*
- *July 17 Nayan was throttled by a biker in Town Hall Square – it's a dangerous place to be!*
- *July 20 I got attacked by a biker - the same one?? - that hit me on the head. Where were we? Nayan and me? We were in…Broughton Astley, yeah, we'd followed the guy.*

-What else is on my list? Oh yeah. Cummings is the surname of Maureen, Mr Gregson's friend from the residential home, who disappeared but left a clue. The clue is a code which I have got written down somewhere, I need to check my notes.

Oh and Nayan's friend Momin is missing too, but that's likely to be nothing to do with any of this, so I haven't put it on the timeline, the same goes for Meera's baby (who isn't missing!).

LIST TWO

Things I know I don't know

- What is Meera's baby called? And what does he look like now?
- What were the results of the DNA test – was it Michael's brother, Steve, in the mortuary?
- Why were Nayan, Michael and me attacked?
- Has Maureen Cummings turned up?
- Has Michael decided whether to contact his biological mother?

LIST THREE

Things I don't know I don't know

Well obv this has nothing on it! Do you think I'm totally crazy???! LOL

LIST FOUR

Things I don't know I know

I'm putting the Code in my blog. Here it is:

'H/16A/85S/92I/86N'

I'm sure I know the answer, I'm sure I worked it out, but what was it??? What did I think it meant?

Did I work it out or did I just dream it? Those people who say you should write down your dreams are on to something, you never know what you might learn!

Let me think for a bit. Need more rest for my brain cells! CYL.

Chapter

16

"Our only chance of long term survival, is not to remain inward looking on planet Earth, but to spread out into space."

Stephen Hawking, 2010

Wednesday, 30th July 2014 11am

Rita is pleased to see the baby, who, she learns, has a name now - Theeran, meaning 'brave' ("Because he has been a brave little soul!" Mrs Shah tells everyone proudly). Meera brings him into Rita's house and hands him to Priya while she fetches the buggy from her car; Priya carefully carries her new nephew into the living room at 10 Elm Drive. His tiny face has a serious expression as if he is really concentrating on all this living business. His body is floppy and fits easily into the shape of Rita's as she takes him from Priya and cradles him against her shoulder, Meera having put a cloth between them ("He's prone to being sick a lot, it's part of him being early. Oh look he's gone to sleep! He must feel comfortable with you Rita.") The tiny frame slumbers on as the two friends discuss developments while Meera looks online for items for her new post- baby wardrobe.

"I've some things to ask you!" Rita announces.

"Go on?" Priya sounds cautious as she sits next to her friend and slumbering nephew, his entire body relaxed, his head heavy against Rita.

"The DNA results." Rita says, "Do we know if Michael and the mystery man are related?"

"So you remember that business!" Priya is pleased. "Yes, indeed, the DNA results show they are, or were, identical twins."

"It is Michael's brother then, what was he called again? Steven? Is that helping the police? To find out what happened?"

"Yes-ish." Priya says unhelpfully. "It means they have a name, which is something, but from what Sergeant Griffiths said, last time I spoke to him, it was proving difficult to find anything about Steve, he's not on any official records. But it's early days I s'pose."

"Well, without you they would have no clue." says Rita, "At least it's a starting point. And has Michael said anything about contacting his birth mother?"

"I haven't heard from him since he went home with his parents." Priya tells her. "I don't know what he is thinking about that."

"Oh, okay." Rita files away the information and thinks she may ring Michael herself, she has his mobile number after their encounters in the Infirmary.

"And Maureen Cummings. Do we know what happened to her?" is Rita's next question.

"You are doing well!" Priya is impressed, "I'm afraid it's not good news. A woman's body was found in the river, the river Soar, near Abbey Park? They found her the same day you were attacked, actually. The care home identified the body as belonging to Mrs Cummings. Her daughter is coming over for the funeral."

"How sad." says Rita, adding "The Soar runs past the Space Centre, could there be a connection?" as the baby stirs slightly and he is passed back to his mother who cocoons him in a sling.

"I'm taking him for a walk." says Priya's sister.

"Shouldn't you be resting?" asks Rita who is sure she has read that rest is important for nursing mothers.

"No, I want to get my figure back!" Meera returns. "Rest is for whimps!" Then, as she leaves, she tells Priya "I'll be back for you in an hour." And then the two are gone, leaving behind a faint smell of baby cream mixed with Meera's perfume.

"That leaves the Code!" says Rita enthusiastically.

Rita and Priya settle at the table in the kitchen to look at her iPad where she has a copy of the code left by Mrs Cummings.

"I'm sure I cracked it before my head got cracked." says Rita. "Or maybe just afterwards. I remember thinking I knew the answer."

"Keep wracking what's left of your brains." encourages Priya.

Rita stares at the message and ponders it yet again just as Nayan appears. He strolls over to put an arm round his sister, still relieved to see her behaving normally again. As he turns he sees the screen.

"What's this? A sudoku?" he asks.

"No silly, it's the code Maureen Cummings left for Mr Gregson!" Nayan is pleased to hear Rita laughing again.

"Hang on!" Rita thinks she has seen something. "What if it's a phone number?"

"Doesn't look like one." says Priya.

"No, but the Leicester code is 0116 right?" Rita persists.

"So?" Priya remains unconvinced.

"Well what if we use the 16 as part of that code, that makes 0116 859286." Rita continues.

"Well it looks like a number!" Priya has to concede, thinking that Rita may be onto something.

"Shall we try it?" Rita reaches for her phone, but before she can press the numbers Nayan snatches the tablet from her, yelling "Bazinga!" (he has been watching back-to-back episodes of *The Big Bang Theory*).

"Oi, what are you doing?" his sister protests.

"Well look at the numbers and think about it!" says Nayan.

"What on earth do you mean?" Rita is sceptical.

"Atomic numbers." her brother says.

"Well? What does that mean?" Rita thinks she should know this, but the effort of recalling it is too much at the moment.

"You know, each element on the periodic table has an atomic number." Nayan explains.

Rita nods, yes, she vaguely remembers this.

"Ah." says Priya, whose recall of what atomic numbers are about is better than Rita's. "So what would the numbers be?"

"I think… aha!…" Nayan is looking at a website where the periodic table can be found, together with the atomic number for each element.

"Come on!" says his sister, "Don't keep us in suspense!"

"Well, I don't know what it means." Nayan starts.

The girls sigh, another dead end!

"No no, I mean I do know what it stands for, but I don't know how it helps." Nayan continues,

"Well, clever clogs?" Rita asks him.

"Write this down," Nayan tells Priya "and see if I'm right"

Priya takes her phone and accesses the note pad as Nayan dictates.

"16 is sulphur the symbol for which is 'S'."

"85 is astatine."

"Astatine?" says Rita," who's heard of that?" prompting Nayan to give her a cautionary look," the symbol for which is 'AT'." he continues, ignoring the interruption.

"92 is uranium." he goes on.

"I've heard of that at least." says his sister.

"And the symbol is 'U'." Nayan goes on.

"86 is radon for which the symbol is 'RN'" he pauses,"And that spells?" he turns to Priya.

"It spells Saturn!" Priya says triumphantly

"Hang on!" Rita sees it now." The letters in between the numbers, rearrange them into one word and what do you get?" she asks excitedly.

Now Nayan looks blank.

"Shani! The god associated with the planet Saturn and the Lord of Saturday!" Rita explains as if it is obvious. "Saturn is feared in Hinduism because it takes so long to pass through the constellations, that's why Shani brings sorrow, pain, misery and loss. Appropriate or what?"

"So the clue means what? Saturn? Saturday?" Priya is not sure she is following all this.

"I think she was leading us to Saturn!" Rita puts forward her theory. "Thanks to you, Nayan, we have a real idea what Mrs Cummings meant."

"And that is?" Nayan is still not sure what it all means.

"Well, I'll suggest to Sergeant Griffiths that they search the Space Centre again, and concentrate on anything related to Saturn. She must have meant us to look there!" Rita gets up to use her phone which is on the table. Priya thinks, that's good, Rita is back on form, but what exactly did Mrs Cummings want them to find?

Wednesday, 30th July 2014 3pm

Priya has left with Meera and Theeran. Rita is impatient to hear back from Sergeant Griffiths. He had listened patiently to their theory and promised to arrange a further search of the Space Centre. As a crime scene he said it was a complete nightmare. It was full of gadgets and gizmos; there were six floors of exhibits with hatches and lockers, lots of places to hide things. We've tried using the sniffer dogs but we don't really know what we're looking for."

"Could it be something that Steven brought in? Is there any CCTV of the entrance?" Rita asked him. "Sadly, no." replied the officer. "There should have been but it was broken on the day, see. Often happens, apparently. Ironic isn't it? We can put a man on the moon and try to send a robot to a comet but we can't get CCTV to work when we need it! I'll let you know if there's any news."

Now her phone rings. A number she does not often get a call from.

"Hi, it's Michael."

"How are you doing?" Rita asks him.

"Healing slowly thanks. I hope to be back playing my trumpet again soon, I just need to be in less pain when I breathe in!"

"Poor you!" Rita sympathises.

"So I've decided to do it!" he announces.

"Do what?" Rita queries.

"To try to contact my birth mother." is the suprising answer.

"Well done! If you are sure?" Rita does not want to sound over optimistic about the outcome.

"Yeah, I am." Michael sounds determined.

"And what does your mum think about it?" Rita checks.

"My parents are cool. They say they've been expecting it all my life."

"So how do you go about it? Contact an organisation to help you?" Rita asks Michael.

"Well, you can do it that way." Michael sounds sheepish. "And maybe I will, but first I thought…" he breaks off and for a moment Rita thinks one of them has lost reception.

"What?" says Rita suspiciously.

"Well." Michael is still there, but sounding hesitant. "What if she's out there, waiting to hear from one of us? What if I just try Facebook?" Michael says.

Chapter

17

"If women can be railroad workers in Russia, why can't they fly in space?"

Valentina Tereshkova, Soviet cosmonaut
and engineer, the first woman to
have flown in space, orbiting
the earth 48 times in 1963.

Thursday, 31*st* July 2014 11.30 am

"She'll turn up you know." Rita hears Priya say as she returns to her bedroom with more paint. They have been talking about Morwenna whose whereabouts Rita has been trying to track on social media but with no result. It was as if she had fallen off the end of the earth! It was so unlike Morwenna not to be posting tweets and messages. It was one of her goals in life to get as many 'likes' as possible from her on line 'friends'.

"People don't stay hidden for ever. Look at your Richard III guy – all that time missing and then they find him in a car park. What did you think of the new Centre by the way?" Priya asks her friend as Rita puts down the tray of paint.

"Well, I went to the Silver Shoe on the way." Rita replies, as they coat their paint rollers in the new (stone blue) paint and turn to the wall to apply it, Rita working from the right and Priya from the left; they hope to meet in the middle.

"No way! I don't believe you!" Priya is amazed and for a moment stops rolling, but then realises this causes the paint to drip down the wall untidily so she resumes her rhythm while trying to look sideways at her friend who is calmly moving her paint roller up and down over the once-pink surface.

"Not when it was open, silly!" Rita smiles at her friend's astonishment, "I went past on the way to the Richard III centre and I saw a light was on so I thought why not? No harm in asking."

"Hmmn." says Priya who thinks there can be harm in asking the wrong person the wrong question.

"Well?" she prompts. Her friend cannot make such a surprising statement and then not give her details, she thinks.

"Nothing to tell really." Rita teases, pushing her tongue under her top lip and then grinning. Then as she sees Priya about to protest she quickly adds, "Okay, well I spoke to a waitress, maybe she's an assistant manager, it's hard to tell. She was wiping down the tables and putting the place straight but she was smartly dressed in a black dress."

"Never mind what she was wearing!" Priya is impatient now. "What did she say?" she asks as she replenishes her paint roller from the tray.

"I hope you're not making too much of a mess up there!" the voice of Padma rises up the spiral staircase before Rita can reply.

"Of course not, Mum!" Rita replies breezily, rolling her eyes in Priya's direction. Rita knows the house is Padma's pride and joy, almost her fourth child, and she is anxious not to have it spoiled.

"It's going well." she adds, then to placate her mother further, "You can come and look later!"

"I'll bring up some refreshments in a while." Padma says by way of a truce.

"Great!" Rita shouts back, then resumes her explanation.

"She just said Jed used to work there, behind the bar, he was 'okay' she said, don't know what that means, and that sometimes he would 'bring a girl'." Rita attempts an Eastern European accent, not very successfully, "And then about a month ago he just didn't turn up. 'He let us down' she said, They had no idea where he lived, no contact number that worked –'he give bad phone number' she said - so that seemed to be a dead end."

"Wow!" Priya appreciates Rita's nerve.

"And the Richard III centre? How was that?" Priya knows her friend's interest in history had made her keen for the new visitor centre to open; the bang on the head had not diminished her enthusiasm.

Rita had been impressed with the pristine centre, shining with its newness, created to commemorate Richard III's bloody, muddy death on the battlefield; she read that the building had once been a school named after Alderman Newton, another of the figures on the Haymarket Clock Tower, and that the organisers hope it will receive 100,000 visitors in its first year. The entrance (with the inevitable gift shop) led to a video display where various characters from Richard's life appeared on film, depicted by actors. Anne, his wife, spoke of her life with him, she was the daughter of the Earl of Warwick, known as the 'kingmaker' for his plotting and plans to put various men on the throne, Also in cameo were Richard's brothers, George, Duke of Clarence, who died in suspicious circumstances, and Edward, who was King as Edward IV.

The exhibits told the story of how the Wars of the Roses raged across England, ending with the battle of Bosworth which took place just outside Leicester. Rita learned that in his short reign Richard did significant things as King, putting legislation into English instead of Latin and creating the concept of bail, for example. Richard had marched out proudly from the City on 22nd August 1585 and certain local landmarks were highlighted as associated with him.

According to the findings of the team who had examined the skeleton found in the car park, he had suffered various injuries before and after death consistent with being struck. A plastic copy of the skeleton represented Richard's body among the exhibits so that various features, such as the scoliosis – the curvature of his back- which he suffered from, could be seen. The actual skeleton when found was not complete, she read, the feet having been lost, probably in a development in Victorian times. Lucky they did not disturb him more! she had thought.

Richard had ridden into the middle of the fighting, it appeared, possibly hoping to kill Henry, which would have turned the battle in his favour. The battle was lost when William Stanley weighed in on the side of Henry and not of Richard, having, it would seem, decided which was likely to be the winning side.What happened to Richard after the battle was the stuff of legend and speculation, but some credence could now be given to the story that he was loaded unceremoniously onto a horse and taken to the City where he was buried, probably quite quickly, at the Abbey of Greyfriars, possibly near the high altar. If the grave had been marked this was lost in the dissolution of the monastery but local people seem to have known that he was buried there because, Rita finds, in the late 16th century Robert Herrick had erected a pillar to say 'Here lies the body of Richard III some time King of England'.

Herrick was a Mayor of the City and and Member of Parliament. He built a mansion and garden where Greyfriars Friary had been. His family, Rita discovered, later emigrated to the United States to practice the protestant religion in peace from persecution and the Herrick family in the US have contributed to the restoration and upkeep of the Peace Chapel in the Cathedral, which Rita had also seen. The Cathedral itself contains a plain grey memorial stone placed there in 1982 to commemorate the death of Richard, and the Cathedral will, the following year, thanks to the outcome of a recent court case, be the final resting place of the bones found in the car park.

Rita had moved on through the exhibits until she descended to a peaceful covered cloister with seating all round it and where part of the floor was covered in glass. This afforded a bird's eye view of the very spot where the King's body was found; some medieval tiles, found in 2013, had been placed in the mud which gave some idea of scale as well as giving the lifeless ground some colour. Otherwise it looked like a vegetable patch ready to be dug over and fertiliser applied, but it was astonishing to think how significant that dent in the ground was and what a secret it had held for so many years, Rita had thought. There could not be many small areas of soil which had been or will be stared at so intensely by so many people, she thought.

Across from the cloister was a tea room where Rita had ordered a mint tea while she looked at the pictures of places associated with Richard's march out of the City that fateful day. The site of the Blue Boar Inn on Highcross Street, where Richard had stayed, is now the site of a Travelodge and nothing of its original construction remains. A small part of a grey stone wall is all that remains of Greyfriars Abbey. There are two gateways to the religious district of Newarke which are extant and would have been there in Richard's time, the Magazine Gateway and the Turret Gateway. The medieval Bow Bridge over the River Soar, which Richard would have crossed on his way out and been taken across on his ignominious return, was replaced in 1863 and has the York white rose motif as decoration, she learnt.

Thursday, 31ˢᵗ July 2014 1.00pm

The girls have eaten the food supplied by Padma and are using the rollers to apply 'Pavilion Gray' when the decorating is disturbed by a call from Sergeant Griffiths which Rita puts on loud speaker while the paint rollers are placed in the tray.

"Just keeping you up to date, Rita. I worry if I don't tell you things that you'll be haring off on another of your jaunts and end up in hospital again!" The girls smile at each other.

"Where has the investigation got to?" Rita asks, pushing her brown curly hair away from her face with her palm and managing to smear a little of the grey paint across her cheek, reminding Priya of the Holi celebrations in Spinney Hill Park earlier in the year when their faces had been streaked with colours.

"We did another search of the Space Centre, as you know." the Sergeant confirms.

"Didn't make us popular like." he pauses for effect.

"And?" says Rita.

"We found a backpack, under the Saturn display, like you thought!"

"Great." says Priya, "Well done Rita."

"What was in it?" Rita wants to know.

"Well, I have to be careful here, ongoing inquiries and all that," Sergeant Griffiths growls in his Welsh accent, "but I can tell you the bag was probably owned by the unknown man." the Sergeant tells them cautiously.

"And his DNA was so similar to Michael's as to show he must have been his identical twin? Steve?" Rita asks impatiently.

"Yes, you were quite right about that." the police officer concedes. "It's given us a few leads to follow, but I have to say there's very little information around about the chap, not even a national insurance number or a benefit claim." Sergeant Griffiths sounds like he is scratching his head for ideas.

"Anyway, the bag" he comes back to the point. "It had in it an annual pass to the Space Centre and some goods that look like they were stolen."

"What sort of goods?" Priya asks, "How do you know they were stolen?"

"There were silver and gold plates and chalices, items that look like they were stolen from churches. The antiques squad are looking in to it now. One of the items was a monstrance."

"A what?" Rita and Priya say together, giving each other baffled looks.

"It's made of metal, they use them in some Christian Churches to display the consecrated host – the bread which is blessed and used in the eucharist? Are you following me?"

"Mmmn." Priya suggests they are just about understanding.

"Well it's not something I'm very familiar with either, to be honest, but this one is spectacular. It looks like a stand with a golden sun on it." The Sergeant goes on.

"A sun?" Rita gasps as a memory slots itself into her head, then she says "Mrs Cummings! Did you say she was found in the river? So sad."

"Yes, we don't know why she left the care home, where she was aiming for, she may have been trying to get to see someone." the Sergeant confirms.

"Or she might have being trying to go back to the Space Centre." says Rita. "Remember Mr Gregson told us she said something about the sun, what was it now?" she pauses, then "Oh yeah!" her eyes sparkle, Priya can see she has remembered, "Maureen Cummings told him that the aliens had given her the sun and she had hidden it. She must have found this bag, don't you think?" Rita asks the police officer excitedly.

"Possibly so," Sergeant Griffiths agrees drily, he has learnt not to leap to conclusions, and to wait for the evidence "Anyway, we're waiting for fingerpint results on the bag. Well done, and I'll keep you informed." and he rings off.

Thursday, 31ˢᵗ July 2014 6pm

The paint is drying. Two grey walls and two blue ones which have transformed the room. When she gets back, Rita will put up her new blind and make up the bed with her new duvet cover, then the makeover will be complete! She feels very satisfied with the changes she has made.

Now Rita has met up with Michael as agreed on the phone ("You will come with me, won't you?"), and the two are entering the foyer of a hotel. Rita can see that he is trembling. A lone figure sits on a chair by the fountain near the reception where counter staff wear shiny smiles like air stewards and glance up and down between computer monitors and guests. The figure stands up and there is something about the way she carries herself that puts Rita in mind of Michael, even though she is shorter and her build is slighter.

Michael and the figure approach each other slowly, like dancers building up to a complicated routine, making cautious, deliberate movements. Then, instinctively, both open their arms.

"Hello Mum." is all Rita hears Michael say before the two are embracing and his mother is either crying or laughing or both.

Rita creeps away quietly, realising her presence is not needed any more.

Chapter

18

"Be opposite all planets of good luck to my proceedings if with pure heart's love... I tender not thy beauteous daughter!"

William Shakespeare,
Richard III Act 4 Scene 4,
spoken by Richard to the widowed
Queen Elizabeth when plotting
to marry her daughter.

Friday, 1st August 2014 9pm

Morwenna is sitting on Jed's shoulders, swaying to the music. Jed is holding her legs, which are draped over him, at the knees, but he does so rather absentmindedly, his concentration focused on the band and on the can from which he sips from time to time.He appreciates the admiring looks which having Morwenna on his shoulders attract from other men in the crowd. It is a good feeling to be envied. If only she would not sway so much; he finds it is hard to keep upright, although possibly the fact that this is his fourth can of the afternoon may be a factor.

Morwenna lifts her arms and swings them to the rhythm of the music which is reaching a climax. Morwenna is glad her kaftan has long sleeves. They hide the rings of bruises on her upper arms where Jed had shaken her during one of his tempers. The bruises have progressed through various colours of purple and yellow and are still obvious. She did not like it when Jed lost his temper, she did not like that he kept her phone, she did not like that he kept her cash card, she did not like that he came and went as he pleased and did not offer an explanation, As she moves to the music Morwenna realises there is not much about the current arrangements that she does like.She smiles at another girl alongside her, also sitting on a man's shoulders, and the girl, who has dark hair tied in a wide red ribbon, and brown eyes, smiles back. She seems happy, Morwenna thinks.

The music is really absorbing; you can lose yourself in it and forget about your problems, Morwenna thinks, as she looks up to the sky, taken up with the sound, the crowd, the moment. She sees a hot air balloon floating in the sky but descending towards them. Will it land on the gig? As the balloon grows bigger, Morwenna can see flame coming from the burner as the balloon is guided closer to the adjacent field. A red white and blue structure, barely skimming and narrowly missing the tree tops, it has a basket suspended below it. As the balloon descends, figures inside it can just be made out. Morwenna catches a glimpse of turquoise. She has definitely seen a turquoise top, she thinks. Suddenly Morwenna feels that help is at hand; she thinks that if she can get to the balloon someone will help her to escape from Jed and her fantasy life, that someone will help her to return to her parents and her 'normal' life. As the song ends and the crowd erupts into applause, cheering and stamping in the mud, she taps Jed on the shoulder. Relieved, he lowers her down, not particularly carefully, and while he puts his hat back on his head Morwennna manages to melt away in the mob and direct herself to the exit into the next field where the balloon basket is just hitting the ground.

Friday, 1ˢᵗ August 2014 7.00pm

The drive to the balloon site in Warwickshire is more nerve wracking than Rita had expected. In his car Jahi conveys his daughter and her friend, Rohan, Nayan and his friend Puli, while Priya's father takes Priya and Ben. The fathers plan to meet up in Stratford-Upon-Avon for a curry while they wait for instructions to collect the passengers. Rita is excited but nervous about what to expect; she has butterflies in her stomach to match the butterfly design on the braid around her favourite long turquoise tunic which she wears over jeans. She has brought a jumper as she is unsure how warm it will be once they are high in the sky and she wonders what that will feel like. Next to her, Rohan's rugged jaw suits the Tigers rugby shirt he is wearing and he grins excitedly at Rita before looking out of the window at the passing scenery while Nayan, in the front of the car, next to his father, has on his Leicester City t- shirt ("to bring us luck this season!").

Priya's father arrives at the airfield just after Jahi and the friends hug as Priya and Ben spill out of his car. Then they walk to the red, white and blue canopy lying beside a basket which is surprisingly large, the size of a small bus. How come they look so small when they are in the sky? Rita thinks.

The organisers welcome them enthusiastically, wearing t-shirts with balloon logos on them and with 'Biggles' style goggles around their necks; they reassure the new customers with slapstick and jokes. A tall, lean, young man with brown stubble on his chin and hair which sticks up at odd angles explains the safety procedures before they climb aboard. The space inside is surprisingly cramped and the 6 of them plus the crew are squashed together. Ben realises that Priya is starting to shake and holds her hand for reassurance. All of them are alarmed at the unsteady feel of the basket but Rita turns to look out over the side of it as the balloon starts to inflate. Now it is happening the butterflies have flown away; she does not want to miss a minute!

The flame which causes the balloon to inflate over the basket is fiercely hot even though, thanks to the safety talk, they are not standing too close to it. As the gas fills out the canopy, the crew release the ropes holding the basket to the ground and it starts to lift up in the air. Rita is amazed how quickly they soar into the sky and the ground shrinks below them. Inside the basket there is a ledge to sit on and after about five minutes or so the friends become more accustomed to the swaying motion, and more confident, and settle to sit on the ledge to enjoy the flight.

Rita feels like she is a gull soaring through the air. It is magical. Warwick Castle can be seen below them to the left and it glows golden in the light of the low sun which is progressing towards setting. Priya's shoulders sink a little as she becomes more relaxed and Ben notices her breathing is steadier now they are in the air, although she jumps a little every time the crew use the burners, which are very noisy in the confines of the basket.

Below them a river looks like a strip of silver paper and the trees look like small plants. The roads are grey lines, but they cannot see any vehicles on them as they are too far away. Clusters of houses make up villages, often surrounding a tall grey spired church. Some industrial estates expand into the fields like silver and blue parcels. Feeling like birds, they are amazed to see real birds swooping and soaring below them. Getting more confident, they take selfies and film each other, smiling and laughing at this memorable adventure.

All too soon for Rita, the crew prepare the balloon for its return to earth. They have explained that the exact landing site will not be known as it depends on the temperature and the wind direction. ("Most farmers don't mind if we land in their field so long as we clear up after ourselves.") The balloon is being tracked using GPS and the plan is for a minibus to collect them all as soon as possible after landing and take them to the rendezvous point where Jahi and Priya's father will be waiting.

As the basket descends it seems to be sailing close to the top of the trees. They all take up the position they were shown in the training, crouching down and holding onto the ropes. Ben and Rohan are tall enough to be able to see over the basket as they come down and exchange a look as they see they are crossing a road and coming very near to a lorry, which beeps its horn, although they are probably about 10 feet above it. Then they can see what looks like a camp site which gets larger and larger until the basket hits the ground nearby as if in slow motion. Priya cannot help crying out in alarm as the balloon touches the ground although she feels very safe with Ben still holding her hand.

"Wow!" says Rita.

"That was awesome!" says Nayan.

"Yeah!" agrees Puli.

"Thanks Rita, that was great!" says Rohan.

They climb up the steps and out of the basket, then they turn to the task of helping to roll up the canopy as they had been instructed. They become aware of a marshmallow pink figure crossing the field, waving its arms at them. Is this an angry farmer perhaps, not happy that they landed in his field? Rita is the first to realise this is someone they know, then Priya, too, recognises the running, booted figure and flowing blond hair.

"Morwenna?" the girls say at more or less the same moment.

"So glad to see you!" Morwenna says breathlessly while Rohan, Ben, Puli and Nayan look on, wondering who this creature could be and where she has come from.

"Please help me Rita! I'm having a terrible time with Jed. I need to get away!" and she sinks to her knees and starts to cry, the depth of her misery not apparent to herself until she had articulated it at that moment.

"Oh Morwenna!" says Priya sympathetically.

"You want to come with us?" Rita asks.

"Oh can I please? I knew straight away when I saw the balloon, I just knew it would be someone who could help. And I saw your top, the turquoise colour, and I just knew it would be you!" Morwenna pours out to everyone's astonishment.

"Well, help us roll up the balloon and we'll see what we can do." says Rita, setting Morwenna to work which she does surprisingly willingly and efficiently while Rita talks to the crew. It turns out there is an extra space in the minibus for Morwenna. Rita asks if they should pay for her but the crew are laid-back and say "Well, if your friend needs help, why not?" Not for the first time, Rita thinks, Morwenna's good looks have probably helped smooth her way.

When the minibus arrives, they clamber aboard, now three girls and four boys, plus the crew, who stow the balloon basket and canopy in a trailer behind the vehicle. Rita calls Jahi to tell him they are on their way to the rendezvous point and that there is an extra passenger to take home.

Saturday, 2nd August 2014 9am

The first things Rita sees when she wakes the next day are Princess Leia and Jar Jar Binks. Is she still in hospital? Is she in another reality, high on morphine again? Or is this a space dream brought on by her visit to the Space Centre? She closes her eyes and opens them again. The princess and the strange creature are still there, as are various white-clad storm troopers, advancing towards her.

Now she remembers, she is sleeping in Nayan's room. Morwenna is in her bedroom and the two brothers are sharing Mohal's bedroom. Morwenna had seemed very upset last night and was not keen to go back to her parents' house. Rita's parents had agreed she could stay the night provided Athena was told she was safe and that she promised to go back the next day after a good night's sleep ("and a good wash" Padma added; 'really the girl looked like she'd been living in a field!' she thought).

Rita uses the shower in the family bathroom, dresses, and knocks on her own bedroom door.

"Come in." Morwenna replies, her voice sounding more in control than it had the previous day.

"Sleep okay?" Rita asks the girl, who is lying in Rita's pyjamas inside Rita's bed.

"Yes thanks." says Morwenna.

"Great." says Rita. "Here's a towel for you to have a shower and I'll find some of my clothes you can borrow for now."

"That's incredibly kind of you!" says Morwenna. "I really don't deserve..." and she bursts into tears.

"Come on." says Rita, giving her a hug. "It can't be that bad. Your Mum and Dad will be so relieved to see you, you've no idea how worried they have been!"

"Oh I know." Morwenna says "I want to see my mum too. So much. But, oh Rita, I'm scared."

"Scared of what? Everything'll be all right now. Your parents will sort out about your phone and your bank account." (Bits of Morwenna's story had tumbled out of her during the minibus ride the previous evening.)

"It's not just that." Morwenna wails, "It's what kind of person Jed turned out to be and I think, I think, I might be pregnant!" and her gentle tears turn into a flood as the girl sobs in Rita's arms.

Saturday, 2nd August 2014 10am

The girls sit at Padma's white kitchen table, Rita tucking into instant porridge, Morwenna playing with her spoon in a bowl of muesli. ("You must eat something, keep up your strength." Padma had insisted before she left for the dental surgery where private patients are seen on a Saturday morning.)

"Do you really think you might be pregnant?" Rita broaches the subject.

Morwenna nods forlornly. "I haven't had a period for a couple of months which isn't like me."

"Okay." Rita swallows some porridge. "Then you have to

do a test. You have to know one way or the other."

"Yeah." Morwenna reluctantly agrees.

"We'll go together, there's a pharmacy down the road."

"Oh no, Rita." says Morwenna "That would be way too embarrassing. Let's go to a pharmacy in town, a big one like Boots, where no one will know us."

"All right." Rita agrees, wondering at what point in the day Morwenna envisages meeting up with Athena, whose problem this should really be.

"And Jed? Tell me more about him. I saw the bruise marks on your arm by the way." Rita probes.

"Yeah, he could be rough some times, when he lost it. You know I saw Jed attack Nayan in Town Hall Square? I stopped him actually. He'd really lost it that day." as Morwenna speaks, Rita becomes wide-eyed with surprise.

"That was Jed? Nayan could hardly speak for days, not that that was a bad thing!" Rita jokes to lighten the mood.

"He just kind of flipped, you know? Especially after that business at the Space Centre."

"The Space Centre?" Rita drops her spoon in astonishment. "What's that got to do with it?"

"I dunno really. There was a day when he came back in a terrible mood. He'd been to the Space Centre to meet his mates and collect something. Only it wasn't there. At least I think that's what he said. He got back really late, after midnight, and then he was on my phone all night saying things like: 'He shouldn't have double-crossed us, we're talking a lot of gear here and where the hell – sorry Rita - could it be?' That's why he attacked Nayan when he did. He thought he knew something about whatever was missing."

"You need to tell the police about this" Rita says "We'll go into town for a pregnancy test and then we'll call on Sergeant Griffiths." she asserts, picking up her spoon to finish her porridge, which is starting to stick to the bowl.

Chapter

19

"All of us have cause to wail the dimming of our shining star"

> Gloucester on the death of
> Clarence in Richard III
> by Shakespeare Act 2 scene 2.

Thursday, 14th August 2014 10am

"Weird, isn't it? That we're going to uni?"

Rita and Priya are hugging each other and jumping up and down at the same time. Reunited outside their school, they know from having checked their UCAS status on line in the early hours that they have scored enough points in their A-levels to secure their university places: Priya to study medicine at Oxford, Rita to read history at Warwick. Entering the school building will enable them to confirm their exact results and, more importantly, to share the joy with those who got their places and to sympathise with those who did less well than expected.

"Pupils who did better than predicted can trade up this year." they overhear Mr Thatcher, a history teacher, telling a parent in the hall "The leading universities have about 3,000 places available through clearing and are competing for the brightest students" Rita hears the teacher say. According to him there are many places being offered for law, maths, physics, chemistry and engineering. Rita thinks back to what happened to her brother ,Mohal, 3 years ago. His results had been worse than expected, and that year there were no suitable places available through clearing, so he took a gap year while he applied afresh. Student fees were different then, too, £6000 not the £9000 they can charge now, and there was no race to secure the brightest in the way that existed now.The removal of any cap on the number of the brightest students, allowing the universities to expand, had led to 'sales gimmicks' like offers of cash, computers and cut-price accommodation.To compound this, Rita has seen on the internet, unis with places to fill had been tweeting the price of alcohol in their area and asking existing students to 'recruit a friend for £200'.

The TV news is on in the main hall, where pupils who are milling to get their results can see their emotions reflected at other schools. Some dance and shout with joy or confirmation (Shouting "Yes" and punching the air is a common response). The more despondent ones are led by teachers to a quieter area or room where their options can be considered. According to the TV coverage, Rita and Priya are among almost 400,000 students accepting university places before A-level results day – a record high. Rita notices a teenager who has gained 11 A-levels at A* and A grades and is going to do PPE at Oxford (that's just showing off, she thinks, no one needs that many A-levels!).

Pupils take selfies with friends and teachers or phone family with their grades. On the TV news Mary Curnock Cook, Chief Executive of UCAS, is saying that demand for university is as high as ever despite a slight fall of 18 year olds in the system. Someone else explains the levelling off of grades this year comes from the abolition of exams in January. This is a transitional year, but the effect of the changes is already being felt. From 2015 (so Nayan will be affected, Rita notes) A-levels will be wholly assessed by end of year exams after 2 years in the 6th form and not by modules or course work as has been possible in the past. For the first time on record, maths is the most popular subject and there is an increase in the numbers choosing science subjects which pleases business leaders. The total of undergraduates starting degrees is expected to exceed half a million for the first time when all places are confirmed, a reporter says.

"Laters." the girls say as they leave the hall, knowing they will meet again in the town centre that afternoon.

Thursday, 14th August 2014 3pm

"Do you think he will come?" Rita asks Priya as they stand at the edge of a group of onlookers gathered in Town Hall Square in Leicester; the crowd are enjoying the music from a busker who is playing a selection of jazz and pop tunes on the trumpet. Rita glances across the crowd, some of whom are swaying to the sound of 'Fly Me to the Moon'. The gathering includes people well- known to Rita and Priya. Athena Maitland is there, together with her husband, Edward, and their daughter, Morwenna who, Rita knows from her text, has secured a place at Exeter University to study English and who (phew!) was not pregnant after all. Next to them is an elderly man in a wheelchair who is Mr Gregson, and behind him stands a careworker, a tall pale young man with curly hair which sits like an ill-fitting tea cosy on top of his head. Meera and her mother stand either side of the buggy holding the newest member of the Shah family. In among the group there also figures who Rita knows are neither relatives nor friends. They are plain clothes police officers.

Priya wrinkles her nose and runs her fingers through her long dark hair arranged today in two bunches which frame her oval face. Wearing a mauve top over white leggings, and canvas shoes, she shrugs her shoulders non-committally in response to her friend's question, not allowing Rita to see how anxious she feels about what might be about to happen. Priya smiles nervously at Ben who is on her left. Rita sighs, disliking the anticipation for different reasons to Priya's, she is impatient to see how things will unfold.

Like many days this summer, the weather is warm and

Rita finds it pleasant to feel on her face an occasional splash of water gushing from the mouths of lions in the fountain which rises proudly in the centre of the Square. She has pushed her brown hair back from her round face with a red band; this matches the colour of her shirt which she wears over a long red skirt, much cooler than leggings she thinks.

On Rita's other side in the crowd, now singing along to 'When You Wish Upon a Star', are her brothers, Nayan and Mohal, both of whom stand several inches taller than her five foot five, their figures contrasting with each other. Mohal, in a blue t- shirt, his dark hair slicked back with gel, has the well-defined chest and strong shoulder muscles of a 21 year old who spends time in the gym. Nayan, five years younger, has straggly strands of brown hair hiding part of his face and his thin figure is exaggerated by a black t-shirt which hangs over his ripped jeans; in one hand he holds a skateboard. As the staccato sound of an approaching motorbike engine starts to interrupt the music, Nayan unconsciously moves nervously nearer his older brother.

"Here we go." Rita whispers into Priya's ear. Not one but two motor bikes roar towards the Square, their riders clad in black and leaning back casually in contrast to the serious machines they are steering, their black helmets, one with a skull and crossbones motif on it, reflecting the bright sun. The trumpet music moves on to 'Moon River' as Rita watches the busker nod in the direction of a smartly dressed black couple, older than he is, who are standing at the front of the crowd and then turns and nods to a single black woman standing slightly apart from the group.

A member of the gathering detaches from the crowd and walks towards the bikers who are parking their vehicles under trees on one side of the Square. At this movement the police officers step out of the group, apparently casually, and take up positions in the Square. The riders have dismounted and taken off their helmets. One has a blue scarf tied on his head and, judging by the pink shade of his face, he may have caught the sun; he walks behind the other who has shoulder length black hair which he wears in a ponytail; he has heavily tattooed arms emerging from the sleeves of a black t-shirt.

The tattooed biker and the person from the crowd exchange words but Rita cannot hear what they say above the raucous singing of the crowd ('Blue Suede Shoes'). While he talks, the biker with the blue head-covering looks anxiously around the Square, gesticulating with his arms in an exaggerated manner when he sees the busker. The man says something and raises his arm, but it is arrested by a police officer who comes up behind him and a shiny metal object clatters to the ground. The man struggles and tries to dodge to his right;he is checked by another police officer and working together the two officers cuff his hands behind his back and turn him towards a police car which has speeded to the Square during the struggle.

Meanwhile the biker with the tattoos lurches forward as if to grab hold of his interlocutor from the crowd, who, clad in a kaftan, steps deftly away to be quickly swallowed back into the audience who are now singing to Elton John's 'Rocket Man'. The biker looks around the Square desperately, like a trapped animal seeking a means of escape, charges towards the officer in front of him, head down, and knocks him over, tipping him backwards into the water of the fountain. The biker manages to stop short of the water's edge himself and avoids falling in, but his forward momentum prevents him from changing direction quickly enough to avoid another officer diving to the ground behind him and grabbing him by the knees. Although weighed down by the officer, the biker tries to move to his right but the policeman holds on and eventually his prey keels over onto his side like a felled tree. A police woman appears and applies handcuffs as she carries out the arrest.

The busker, a black man in his late twenties wearing grey

trousers, a white shirt and a waistcoat, seems to shake his head a little as he comes to the end of the song and shakes out his trumpet before starting on his next tune.

"Everything will be all right now." Rita tells Priya as the bikers are driven away and the trumpet player strikes up *Lady in Red*.

Chapter

20

"The weary sun hath made a golden set, and by the bright track of his fiery car gives signal of a goodly day tomorrow."

Richard III by William Shakespeare,
Act 5, Scene 3, Bosworth Field,
words spoken to Richard by Richmond.

Saturday, 16th August 2014 12pm

"Form up! Charge!"

Horses and men clatter towards and then through one another, rolling and striking out in the mud as they dismount, their silver-grey chainmail grimy. The battle is not glamorous. The men are not noble knights on a quest. They can be heard breathing heavily and their spittle can be seen dripping down their tunics. The swords are not the finely-honed pieces of steel seen in television costume dramas but flat, hard, grey strips of metal, as useful for hitting a man over the head as for stabbing him. But no one actually dies today. Rita and Priya are at Bosworth field for a re-enactment to mark the 529th anniversary of the battle there (or in fields nearby, the exact location is the subject of some discussion among historians who have made recent finds of cannonballs which suggest the traditional site may not be the right one exactly, but the picnickers don't seem to mind). Padma has packed bagels, falafels, carrot sticks, hummus and yoghurts, while Nayan has brought chocolate bars and Mohal contributes cans of apple juice to complement the bottles of water packed by Padma. To witness the event together are gathered the Patel and Shah siblings with other family and friends.

During a lull in the hostilities ("I don't suppose they stopped for lunch in the real battle." says Mohal) the party sits around a picnic cloth. Morwenna is in her now-trademark kaftan and long boots and has recovered from the nerve-wracking encounter with Jed in Town Hall Square, Priya and Rita wear jeans and ankle boots with bright t-shirts (Priya's yellow, Rita's turquoise). Nayan's friend Zeedan wears his penguin t-shirt. Meera and Jai take the opportunity of not holding their baby to help themselves to food while they can. Mrs Shah cradles her new grandson in her arms proudly, ("See he is smiling at his grandmother!" she says).

"Mo's mother has gone to Syria, to try to get him back," Nayan tells Rita as they sit down together.

"Really? How crazy! I guess she's desperate." Rita replies.

"She thinks he's just made a mistake. She says he's only a kid. He's never been out of the country on his own. The family came here from Bangladesh. They've worked hard to give the boys a good home. They can't understand it."

"Mmmn" says Rita, chewing on a carrot stick, "But if you look at some of his brother's tweets you can get their dissatisfaction. 'Sometimes I get sick of this life. I'm livin to eat, study, work, pay tax, sleep #Slave.' " she quotes.

Nayan nods, he too has read the passages from the Twitter account which seem to show the brothers' attitude.

"Well he's a slave now. Of a different sort!" says Rita.

"But from what I've seen on Twitter, he can't leave. ISIS have taken his passport he says." Nayan is concerned.

"Doesn't sound too hopeful for him being able to come back then." Mohal joins in from the other side of Rita.

"If he does make it back, can he be charged with something?" Nayan wants to know. "People have been talking about treason!"

"That goes back to a law made in 1351." Rita explains, "I think we are in danger of getting as medieval as the terrorists!"

"So what is treason anyway?" Priya asks her from across the picnic.

"It is to 'levy war against our Lord the King' – obviously the Queen now - in his realm or give the king's enemies comfort elsewhere.'" Rita explains, "Sounds wide?" she offers her opinion.

"Yes, but get real!" Mohal again "Do we want jails full of angry fundamentalists? Wouldn't it be better if we could re-educate them? That's the route the Dutch are taking and they always seem more moderate about these things, Look how they reacted when that plane was shot down carrying mostly people from Holland. Dignified or what?"

"How will Mo's mother get to Syria?" Morwenna queries from next to Priya, her knowledge of geography being shaky despite her father's frequent trips abroad.

"Via Turkey I gather." Nayan supplies the answer "She's gone out there with changes of clothes."

"Well good luck to her!" Mohal again, "She's a brave woman!"

"Oh, hello!" Rita stands to greet Michael and his biological mother, Carol, late arrivers at the battlefield.

When they are settled round the picnic cloth with a drink and a plate of food ("We need to eat it all, Mum will be disappointed if we take anything back!") Michael speaks.

"So Sherlock and Watson." he addresses Rita and Priya, "Tell us what the police have found out about what went on at the Space Centre."

"Well, clearly everything is subject to the court process, those we think were involved are pleading not guilty so the case has to be proved." Rita tells him cautiously.

"Great! Can we go and see the trial?" Nayan is keen, while others shake their heads and Morwenna shivers at the thought. It is possible she will be asked to give evidence as Jed is claiming her as an alibi for times when he was not with her.

"When will any trial be?" Morwenna now asks.

"Probably not until early in the new year, according to Sergeant Griffiths." Rita tells her.

"Some of the suspects the police arrested are in custody, the rest are out on bail… Jed's in custody." she adds hastily when she sees the look of alarm on Morwenna's face.

"So what happened to … Steven do they think?" Carol speaks softly, hesitating over the name of her other son.

"Piecing it together, the fingerprints on the goods in the backpack belonged to Steve and to the lady, Mr Gregson's friend, who went missing." Rita tells her, helping herself to a bagel.

"Maureen Cummings" Mohal supplies to Priya's surprise, she had not realised he had been taking so much notice.

"Yes. So the chalices and plates and the monstrance…" Rita continues.

"Monstrance, what's that?" Nayan asks.

"We've been through this." Rita says patiently, "It's for presentation of the host – the consecrated bread used in the Christian eucharist service. It's a beautiful object, all gold and shiny".

"Yes" says Carol, "I think I've heard of it."

"So, anyway" Rita continues "They had been stolen from various churches in the Leicestershire area, there was a spate of burglaries although exactly who did them is still not clear. But the goods were being used to fund the purchase of drugs, that's the police case. There was this guy Jake who was at the centre of it all, using others as couriers to pass the goods and the drugs round the country."

"And Steve was involved in all this?" Michael shakes his head.

"Yeah, sadly he was probably one of the couriers." Rita tells him.

"Oh dear." groans Carol.

"But not out of choice they think." Rita quickly adds.

"How do you mean?" Michael asks.

"Well you've heard about the Modern Slavery Bill going through Parliament?" Rita queries unexpectedly.

"Mmmn." is the general noise mumbled around the picnic. No one is exactly sure.

"I thought that ended years ago? William Wilberforce and all that?" Mohal is prepared to admit his ignorance.

"You might think so, but that's not the case. Steve seems to have been unhappy in various foster homes." Rita pauses when she sees the pained expression on Carol's face, then decides to continue, she will hear this at some point. "And then left care when he was 16. The social workers say they tried to help him set up home in a flat but he didn't seem to know how to look after himself and they are pretty sure he was dealing in drugs even then, although they didn't know it for sure and couldn't prove it."

"And then?" Michael is anxious to know all he can about his brother.

"He just seems to have disappeared. No criminal record, which is why they didn't have his fingerprints on file. At some point, probably quite early on, he came under the influence of this Jake and his family who ran a vegetable farm near Broughton Astley. Some how the people they picked up off the streets, some were vulnerable, some were addicts, were forced to work really long hours for basic accommodation, in caravans, and given just enough to eat. They were probably told they would be shopped to the police if they tried to escape; they may have been brainwashed or become institutionalised."

Rita sees Carol's look of bewilderment. "If only I'd known." she mutters.

"It must have been something like that," Rita goes on, "because it looks like Steve was with them for quite a few years."

"And it's not a criminal offence? To keep people like that?

To treat them so badly?" Nayan this time.

"Well that's why they are passing the Modern Slavery Bill. To put a stop to human trafficking. It's all a grey area at the moment. Obviously there are offences, like assault, but where there is an adult who submits to the arrangements it's hard to pinpoint what the crime is, and the police have certainly not been alert to what has been going on." Rita puts down her bagel.

Everybody sighs. No one is hungry any more. The story is so sad.

"So after working on the farm for a while it seems, from what Jake has told the police…" Rita goes on.

"They found Jake through Jed?" Morwenna interrupts to clarify.

"Yeah." Rita confirms, "According to him Steve was collecting stolen goods and passing them on. Eventually they would reach a buyer and the proceeds would go to Jake who, it seems, although he's not admitting it, would buy drugs for that side of his operation."

"So Steve was at the Space Centre to pass on the goods stolen from churches?" Michael checks.

"If only I could have known what a miserable life he was leading, I would have rescued him!" wails Carol, "But at least we gave him a decent funeral!" she adds recalling the simple ceremony which she had arranged with Michael and his parents; it had seemed the right thing to do.Ben, Rita and Priya had attended, Ben reading the 23rd Psalm ("*The Lord is my Shepherd*").

"Yeah." nods Michael soberly.

"Are drugs still so popular?" Priya asks out of interest for her future profession.

"Oh yes", Rita reaches for her iPad to check some figures. "Sergeant Griffiths told me that according to a recent report by the Centre for Social Justice, Britain has more opiate users than any other European country. More than 380,000 people are regular users of opiates or crack cocaine. What's more some Islamic terror groups are benefitting from the proceeds of the drugs trade. There are routes from the Taliban-controlled opium fields of Afghanistan across the Indian Ocean overland to South Africa. The coasts of Pakistan and Iran have also become gateways for heroin. The drugs come to Britain in container ships. Arms for the terrorists are being paid for by the lines of British people buying their drugs."

"And they make a lot of money? The drug suppliers?" Mohal asks.

"You bet. A kilo of heroin might be worth £450 at the point of origin, £20,000 on entry into the UK and have a street value of £75,000. You can't make that sort of profit easily by lawful means!"

"And how does it get to the users? I've seen dealers on the street, when I've been busking, I guess we all have, but how does it get to them?" Michael again.

"Apparently, it goes to centres like London, Birmingham, Manchester and Liverpool and is then sent by road across the UK. Sergeant Griffiths told me the police have found Pakistani gangs who compete with each other for the business, as well as white criminals with their own networks."

Rita and Morwenna exchange knowing looks, thinking of Jed and his friends. How far they were involved in distributing the drugs they do not know, but it seems possible they had a role since they were also moving the stolen goods around.

"And how do users get it?" Carol this time. "It can't always be on the street?"

"More and more it's via the internet, what they call the 'dark net'" (Mohal seems to know a lot about this, thinks Rita) Her brother goes on "Software is used to mask a person's ID and they log on to websites – you must have heard of the Silk Road website nicknamed an 'eBay for drugs'? As fast as the authorities try to shut it down, another one pops up. People order on line and jiffy bags are sent through the post with several ounces of heroin in them."

"OMG!" Priya is amazed at the situation and at Mohal's knowledge about it, "It's so business-like, like a legit transaction!"

"Criminals use all modern means of communication and distribution I s'pose." Rita replies, "Look at ISIS on social media."

"And drugs are how ISIS get their funding?" Mohal asks.

"The drug trade is part of it, but there are other sources of money I dare say." Rita tells her brother, thinking of the ransom demands reported on the news.

"I don't think Mo and his brother knew that." Nayan puts in. "I hope his mum gets him back."

"So what exactly happened to Steven?" Carol brings the discussion back to her other son.

"Oh yeah." Rita closes her iPad, "So far as the police have pieced it together, he was meant to give the bag with the stolen goods in it to Jed and his friends. And that was his problem. Somehow he lost the bag. Perhaps he put it down or dropped it or put it in a locker and didn't lock it? Whatever happened, Jed says when they came to collect the bag Steve didn't have it."

"So they beat him up?" Mohal asks.

"Tortured him more like!" Priya interjects, Ben, sitting beside her, squeezes her hand. They both recall the marks on the body they saw in the post-mortem examination.

"They were pretty ruthless I'm afraid." Rita confirms. "They were desperate to get the goods. They knew that Jake would blame them if they didn't pass them on as agreed. And they needed the money."

Morwenna nods, thinking of Jed with her bank card.

"But to kill him!" Priya is horrified. "Why would they do that? What would it achieve?"

"Well they didn't know they had, killed him I mean, according to what they told the police. They roughed him up, then gave him some of the heroin to see if he would spill the beans, but he seemed to have a reaction to it – so they say - so they left him to sleep it off in the Mercury Capsule."

"Surely they would realise he genuinely didn't know where the bag was? Why would he have hung about to meet them if he did? He'd have scarpered wouldn't he?" Michael tries to understand the actions of Jed and his gang.

"Who knows what they thought." Rita again, "It sounds like everyone was panicking at this point."

"And then?" Carol prompts.

"Well, when the bikers came back see if the goods would turn up they found the police there. They knew something had gone down but not what. No one said that Steve was dead."

"Which is why they attacked you? In Town Hall Square?" Carol speaks to her son.

Michael turns to her, rubbing ruefully at the scar under his shirt. "Yeah. Like you." he nods to Priya, "When they saw me they saw the resemblance, only they thought I was my brother – the brother I forgot I had - that's why they called me Steve and why they stabbed me."

"I can't believe you went through all that." says Carol

"Well, thanks to Sherlock and Watson." now he is nodding to Rita and Priya together, "The police got involved." Michael raises his eyebrows as he remembers their visits to his bedside, "And I found you." turning to his mother, "So for us it's a happy ending!"

"And your parents, your adoptive parents, how do they feel about it?" Morwenna asks, pleased the attention is focussed now on Michael and not her involvement with Jed.

"They've been great," says Michael. "Really happy to meet up with Carol and show her what a great job they've done with me!" he says immodestly.

"Is Jed being charged with murder?" Priya wants to know, thinking of Morwenna.

"Manslaughter." Rita tells them, "None of the gang will admit who did what, so it's being treated by the police as a joint enterprise."

"What does that mean?" Nayan wants to know.

"It means everyone in a group can be convicted if the police cannot establish which of them actually inflicted the injury." Rita tells him.

"Yeah, little brother," Mohal interrupts, "So be careful who you hang out with!"

Rita frowns and continues,

"It means potentially that all those involved can be charged and convicted if they won't give evidence against each other. It kind of makes sense, but it's tough if what happens is genuinely spontaneous.It's quite controversial." Rita rolls her head from side if side as if weighing up the merits, her brown hair falling untidily around her face as she does so.

"In this case, who knows, but seeing how excited they got when they mistook me for Steve they probably egged each other on, that's what I think, and as a result I lost the chance to meet up with my brother again." Michael says.

"And I never had a chance to get to know him. Maybe if I had I could have saved him." Carol sounds regretful.

"What will happen to the others who were used like slaves, the ones at the farm?" Ben inquires.

"They have been released and social services are helping them to reacclimatise to ordinary life; it won't be easy for them." Rita tells them.

"And the stolen goods?" Priya asks.

"Will be returned to the churches." is the answer.

"So Maureen Cummings was involved?" Mohal shows he is still paying attention.

"Somehow she must have come across the stolen goods by accident. She knew what was in the bag." says Rita "Remember she said to Mr Gregson that she'd been given a present of the sun? She must have got it into her head to hide it and then left the clue in the locker, giving Mr Gregson the key."

"And the police didn't find it?" Ben is sceptical.

"Not at first. Although the police searched the Space Centre it clearly wasn't the easiest of crime scenes. She had hidden the bag well behind the Saturn part of the exhibition. Even with the clue it took a while for the searchers to find it." Rita explains.

"And why did she leave the Home? Where was she going?" Priya queries. "It was a sad end, drowning in the river."

"We'll never know what was in Maureen Cummings' mind. She was a bit confused. The river runs past the Space Centre so it's likely she was heading there. Whatever, she never meant Steve to come to any harm I'm sure." Rita concludes.

The baby stowed in his car seat, and the remains of the picnic in the Peugeot, Rita and Priya wave goodbye to Theeran, Meera, Jai and the proud grandmother. Then they take their leave of Carol and Michael.

"We promise not to trouble you again!" Rita says, "And that goes for Sergeant Griffiths too, he's heard quite enough from us!"

Athena has arrived to pick up Morwenna and she strolls to her mother's car, waving at the others. Mohal takes up the driver's seat in the Peugeot; Nayan climbs in to sit next to him and they set off, Mohal tooting the horn.

Rita is getting a lift in Ben's car with Priya. The remaining three soak up ,one more time, the sunlight of another gloriously bright day.

"We will keep in touch, won't we? And still do all the fun things together?" Priya utters what Rita is thinking.

"We will do Holi together again next year, won't we?" Priya goes on, anxiously,her words bringing to mind the festival enjoyed by about 5,000 people - the food, the bonfire and the colours! She and Rita had green, blue and red daubed over their faces, their clothes later drenched in dye.

"Of course we will!" Rita says confidently.

Rita takes a last look across the battlefield and at the flags flying in the distance which mark the positions of the three forces – victorious Lancaster, vanquished York, vascillating Stanley. Then she, Priya and Ben link arms and march forward together towards the future.

Rita Patel returns in
Body in Grace

ISBN: 978-1-910779-68-2

ISBN: 978-1-910779-69-9

ISBN: 978-1-910779-70-5

ISBN: 978-1-910779-71-2

ISBN: 978-1-910779-72-9

ISBN: 978-1-910779-73-6

ISBN: 978-1-910779-74-3

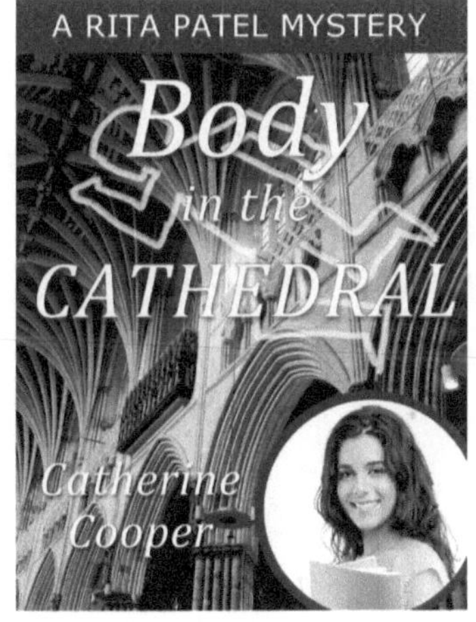

ISBN: 978-1-910779-75-0

www.ingramcontent.com/pod-product-compliance
Lightning Source LLC
Chambersburg PA
CBHW062002190726
48285CB00003BA/959